EVERMORE

EVERMORE

--◄ *By* ►--

BARBARA and DWIGHT STEWARD

WILLIAM MORROW AND COMPANY, INC.

NEW YORK   1978

Printed in the United States of America.

Library of Congress Cataloging in Publication Data

Steward, Barbara.
   Evermore.

   I. Steward, Dwight, joint author. II. Title.
PZ4.S84914Ev   [PS3569.T458]   813'.5'4   77-13768
ISBN 0-688-03278-8

BOOK DESIGN   CARL WEISS

First Edition

1   2   3   4   5   6   7   8   9   10

For

Ted and

Alison Steward—

Evermore

DEATH OF EDGAR A. POE

WE regret to learn that EDGAR A. POE, ESQ., the distinguished American poet, scholar, and critic, died in this city yesterday morning, after an illness of four or five days.—This announcement, coming so sudden and unexpected, will cause poignant regret among all who admire genius, and have sympathies for the frailities too often attending it. Mr. Poe, we believe, was a native of this State, though reared by a foster-father at Richmond, Va., where he lately spent some time on a visit. He was in the 38th year of his age.*

THE SUN
Baltimore
October 8,
1849

* Ed. note. The above account should read: "He was in the fortieth year of his age." Poe was a vain man. When asked his age, he would frequently subtract a year or two. Obviously, many people believed him.

EVERMORE

PROLOGUE

You're in the academic racket. You spend your days teaching college students the difference between a simile and a metaphor. ("No, Mr. Goodhart, it's the other way around.") At night, you aggravate your astigmatism by putting tiny red marks in the margins of a bottomless pile of compositions. Bleary-eyed, in the early morning hours, you toddle off to bed. Yet again stumbling over yet another mound of books. Unaccountably, they seem to increase and multiply of their own volition, threatening to evict you from your cramped apartment. You fall asleep and dream of owning a spacious house, one where a moderate-sized library would feel decently at home.

Appears upon the market a late Victorian pastiche with real imitation Doric columns. It is almost affordable. As befits an absentminded professor, a month elapses before you notice that there is not a single closet on the ground floor. Your books are comfortable, but mufflers, tweedy jackets and rumpled raincoats adorn every chair in sight. You simply must find something to hold the stuff. In a converted barn near the Maryland-Delaware border, you find *it*. Towering above a host of its lesser brethren is a truly monstrous armoire whose unabashed ugliness charms you at once. You pay just over six times the amount you figure it's worth. You should have known. The sign on the door read: JUNQUE.

Of course your pet behemoth does require a little work. Oh well, buy in haste, refinish at leisure. Removing decades of enamel and varnish, you are eventually rewarded with a handsome oak grain. In the process you discover that the funny-looking thing beneath the mirrored door is not just another piece of elaborately carved skirt, but a drawer. Knobs broken off, painted firmly shut, but perhaps still usable. With pliers, screwdriver, a couple of beers and many expletives, you finally work it open and . . . No! You refuse to believe, and pop another beer. Not that staple of the eighteenth-century gothic, the nineteenth-century mystery, the twentieth-century thriller. Not a lost manuscript, for Chrissake! The Angel of the Odd has struck again.

Your discovery is actually an accounts book. Black-and-white marbled boards, maroon cloth spine, measuring fourteen inches in height by twenty-four in width. There are 143 leaves, with indications that several others have been torn out. The pages are a pale green, ruled into ledger columns, vertically and horizontally. The tops of the pages and the gutter margins are marked by a double-line rule in red. The first eleven leaves are filled with dates (month and day only, no year) followed by notations of expenditures and receipts. These are entered in a careful, precise hand in black ink, quite legible, with no blots or corrections.

On the recto of the twelfth leaf, however, you find written in a spidery script: *Wilmot Rufus Griswold—A Memoir.* The lines which follow are scrawled across the full width of each page, obviously written in haste. Blots and crossed-out words are frequent. Pink stains appear on several leaves. The memoir runs uninterrupted to the verso of leaf 135. The remaining leaves are blank. Between the last leaf and the backboard is a piece of heavier paper with a rough finish, measuring some fifteen inches square. It is folded into quarters and at its center the creases break the substance of the paper itself. It is an unsigned charcoal sketch of a man's face, done with some skill, but marred by a scribbled hairline and moustache.

On a whim, you decide to prepare a readable text of the Griswold memoir. What the hell, it beats finishing the article for PMLA you started, the one in which you learnedly discourse on the significance of the frequency of periodic sentences in Milton's early prose. Problems abound. For example, in his haste, Griswold resorts to abbreviations, writing *Wh.* for *what, which,* or *who.* His spelling is erratic: Mallarmé is variously rendered as *Mallame, Malarme,* or *Malarm.* Griswold exhibits a sublime indifference to diacritical marks. Whether the language is French, German, or Hungarian, he simply refuses to use them. And, like many memoirists, the author omits quotation marks to set off direct discourse. To supply them when three or more speakers are involved proves a challenge. On occasion, entire passages defy interpretation and must be omitted.

Further, you are driven to make some alterations simply to preserve a reader's sanity: Griswold—it is soon learned—was overly fond of the dash—which—when combined with his ornate—indeed, pompous—literary style—might occasion difficulties—if not incomprehensibility—in any attempt—by even the most dedicated reader—to fathom his meaning. Amen. You yearn for the easy concision of Milton, but persevere until the task is completed.

You then find that transcribing the memoir is only the beginning. The tale is so bizarre (to use one of Griswold's favorite words) that it defies credibility. Yet the tone and style of the memoir suggest a man struggling to report truthfully events that he has witnessed. Was there really a Wilmot Rufus Griswold? According to the City of Baltimore, no. "That doesn't mean nothing," says a clerk. "Back then people got born and died without fussing over pieces of paper." What of the Griswold Medical Dispensary? "Well, they made a lot of things in those old buildings out on Frederick Street. Some of them even blew up. But there's no company by that name that I can find."

There are still Griswolds in Baltimore, of course, but no record in any family history of a Wilmot Rufus Griswold. You are not downcast, however. Once upon a graduate course, you encountered the so-called authorized biography of Edgar Allan Poe written by Rufus Griswold, Wilmot's reputed uncle. It was a thoroughly shoddy piece of work for which the elder Griswold forged documents to support his lies. Thus, the role assigned Rufus Griswold in the younger Griswold's memoir is, you decide, entirely believable.

You badger librarians for other source materials by and about Poe. These are checked and cross-checked. Poe did meet General Winfield Scott at West Point. He wrote of the meeting in a letter of 6 November 1830, at the same time begging his foster father John Allan for money. In 1843, at his own expense, Poe did reprint "The Man that Was Used Up." And Poe's correspondence is studded with references to "Muddy," his familiar name for Mrs. Maria Clemm, his mother-in-law (with whom, according to Rufus Griswold, the poet had "criminal relations"). Finally, Poe was placed under the care of Dr. J. J. Moran at Washington Hospital in Baltimore. But the Doctor's romantic account of Poe's death-bed conversion is absurd.

In fact, every reference to the life and death of Edgar Allan Poe made by Griswold can be verified—up to that fateful day in October, 1849.

At the Baltimore Historical Society's library, you discover that politics during the period in question were rather colorful. One delightful message from the past sticks in your mind: ". . . then the Whigs captured a cannon which had been brought to the city by the militia in an attempt to restore order. For several hours they rained shot down upon a vast area, preventing voters from reaching the Polls." And later, with understandable smugness, a journalist notes: "The election of 1860 was a peaceful one. Not a single person was shot."

You dig up, almost literally, an antiquarian who proudly displays a moldering cloth banner which, he informs you, was hung across a Baltimore street in the election of 1849. On the banner is printed: THE FOURTH WARD IS AWL RIGHT! A quaint misspelling, you observe naively. And you receive a lecture on the humble shoemaker's awl, the most potent force in American politics for nearly a century. The procedure was simple. A prospective voter for another party approached the polling place. A cry went up: "Give him the ice," or "Put him on the ice." The hapless participant in democracy was then surrounded by a crowd of bystanders, all apparently clamoring to vote, and everyone of them armed with an awl. As the surge receded, the poor voter found himself quite severely punctured and quite incapable of voting. Triumphantly you reason that this would certainly account for the wounds which Le Rennet describes to Griswold.

You sneak off to Washington for a few days and plod through the State Department archives. Joy! Jared Rathbone was the U.S. Consul in Paris during the Exposition of 1889. Gloom. Rathbone's scant personal papers and his voluminous official reports fail to mention either Wilmot Rufus Griswold or Henri Le Rennet.

Perversely your determination to prove or disprove the authenticity of Griswold's narrative grows. You delve into the material on the Mayerling affair. Nearly a century has elapsed since the deaths of Crown Prince Rudolph and Baroness Mary Vetsera at the imperial hunting lodge. The mysterious circumstances surrounding the incident have been catalogued, examined, debated. True to their nature, scholars of the subject have agreed to disagree on almost everything except the fact that the deaths occurred. Yet the facts related by Griswold are supported by any number of independent accounts. References to the personal letters and papers of Crown Prince Rudolph are generally accurate—although Griswold apparently had lapses of memory now and again. (A letter written by Rudolph to his tutor, for example, is described as being addressed to his mother.) Even Father Degrote's story is authentic. In the Political Archives of the Ministry of the Imperial Household, Vienna, there are dusty folders labeled THE PARRAMATTA MYSTERY.

The evidence mounts, and you become absolutely convinced of the document's authenticity—on Monday, Wednesday, and Friday. On Tuesday, Thursday, and Saturday, you are equally convinced that the whole thing is a hoax. On Sunday, you vacillate and putter with Milton's prose. Blessed summer arrives. ("Goodbye, Mr. Goodhart, and good luck.") You decide to take a flyer and arrange a working vacation in Paris. After all, Paris was the locus of the incidents described by Griswold and verification might be found.

And in the beginning, it seems you *might* be successful. Yes, you discover, from rue de Rome, Griswold could have easily heard a train whistle. And starting in the general area of St. Germain des Pres, the walk to Baudelaire's grave would fall within the length of time attributed by Griswold to his ghostly midnight stroll. Yes, the American dentist, Thomas Evans, was a well-known figure in Europe during the last half of the nineteenth century. Although no record exists of his treating Empress Elisabeth, he did number Louis Napoleon and Empress Eugénie and other royalty among his patients. In a gallery you study a painting by Edouard Manet. Yes, Mery Laurent, a little younger then, but essentially as described by Griswold. And she obviously possessed the worldly sensuality which would have overwhelmed a middle-aged man from Baltimore on his first trip to Paris. The French police? Everyone is polite. But about your inquiries concerning, ah, let us see, a M. Le Rennet and a M. Griswold. They smile and shake their heads.

Considerably poorer and but little wiser, you return to the groves of academe. You collect bits and pieces of fact, rumor, coincidence. Two shoeboxes of note cards expand to fill a file cabinet. You procrastinate. The Milton article languishes. Finally, you take the leap of blind faith recommended by Pascal. You approach a New York editor with the manuscript. Very interesting, you are told. Could you return in a week? You could. You do. "Most fascinating," he swears. "But I'm afraid I just couldn't risk publishing this without more documentation." You are thanked profusely for allowing him to read the memoir. As you exchange pleasantries and prepare to leave, he drops the bomb. "As I say, I couldn't publish this, but perhaps our fiction department . . ."

Delicious. An irony which Poe himself would have loved.

BARBARA and DWIGHT STEWARD
September, 1977

THE

GRISWOLD MEMOIR

CHAPTER

1

*. . . to the earth art thou not
for ever dead?*

ODEON! MONTMARTE! PIGALLE! TO A NATURE MORE RO-
mantic than my own, these very names might occasion the
most extreme flights of fancy, of tantalizing expectations, of
dreams lying await around each corner. Personally, I found
the streets of Paris confusing, noisome, and filled to overflowing with rude, jabbering people. I was constantly losing my
way, since it is apparently against municipal law and popular
custom for those streets to proceed in a single direction for
any length worth measuring. And why are the good citizens
of that metropolis never *satisfied* with their streets? Relentless
as the Furies, pavers tear up the cobblestones, and after allowing them to stand heaped for several days, they pound them
down again—with little discernible improvement, I must add!
How unlike my own noble Baltimore, "That city enchanting!
In the distance away, roll the foam-crested waves of the
Chesapeake Bay," *et cetera*. Yet because of one of those
wretched streets—a street whose name I was never to learn—
I met him, and became involved in the *affaire* Mayerling.

It began in all innocency on a Saturday night, February

second, 1889. With some recent acquaintances, I attended what the French call a *reveillon* at a garish restaurant, Maxim's. Although we talked of the coming trade exposition, our most absorbing topic was whether the next century would begin on January 1, 1901, or on January 1, 1900, as I maintained. The debate was accompanied by several bottles of wine, my inordinate consumption of it resulting, I believe, from the extraordinarily disputatious nature of my French friends. My recollection of pursuant conversations and frivolities is cloudy, but that they were exceedingly boisterous there can be no doubt.

Of a sudden and to my chagrin, I awakened to an empty room. A waiter, his hand still on my shoulder, pressed *l'addition,* as the French say, into my hands. The charges for broken china and crystal nearly equalled the cost of our dinner and libations. Too weary to argue, I donned my Kitchener overcoat and genuine Baltic seal *chapeau.* Yet once outside, having gulped draughts of fresh air, face dampened by the falling snow, I was sufficiently invigorated to hire a cab and rejoin my friends. In the company of some ladies, they had departed to continue their celebration elsewhere, having left for me an address scribbled on a napkin, for which, I might add, I had been charged on that immense bill.

The cabbie was no less exorbitant in his demands, but, I philosophized, this was my first exposure to *la vie Parisienne,* and knowledge of the world is seldom without cost. I alighted, the driver pointed, and, touching his whip to the flank of his steaming horse, he sped away. The pleasant mood engendered by my reflections disappeared as rapidly as he. Thirty-nine rue Croix des Petit Champs was the address of the Banque de France. Apparently one of my companions had made a mistake when he copied the number and street on the napkin.

Weary again and feeling a touch dyspeptic, I determined to return to my hotel. With no cab in sight, I had to walk. The beacon atop the still incomplete Eiffel's tower, ahead and to my right, served as a guide. A poor one, as it proved. Lost in a swirl of snow and a muddle of streets, I was soon hopelessly out of my reckoning. My relief, therefore, was profound when I heard the clatter of a cab. He slowed and stopped. Joyously, I ran across the snow-mantled road. My left foot plunged into a hole, so that, pitching forward, I fell onto a heap of those damnable cobblestones and damaged my teeth. I cursed, forgetting the words of the Attic sage: things are where things are, and as Fate has willed, so shall they be fulfilled.

It was not until midday on Monday that I felt my left ankle and bruised body were strong enough to carry me from my hotel bed to a dentist, whose attention my mouth desperately demanded. Without wishing to disparage the solicitous care of the hotel porter and his wife, I might say that my head had been further jarred by their continued arguments over the efficacy of Bromo Vichy, herb teas, Carbo wafers, Angel's Oil, Blackberry Balsam and other specifics of a French household's pharmacopeia.

Leaving my ice pack behind, I limped off to a dentist whose offices were in our *arrondissement*, a shocking and futile venture. Babbling affably, exuding the odor of wine, the dentist rolled his grimy sleeves above his elbows and slipped into a blood-spattered apron.

"*Allons!*" he called, grinning insanely.

I fled. In my agony and despair, I sought assistance and refuge in the only sure harbor that I knew, and, miraculously having negotiated a labyrinth of twisted streets, I found it. Holds the world a sight so stirring! so inspiring! so comforting! as The Stars and Stripes! Proudly I flung back my shoulders. Despite my gait being stiffened by my injured ankle, I marched, head high, down a walkway lined with sapling pine trees. Gratefully, I entered through the brass-bound portals of The American Consulate.

After a considerable wait, the Consul General, Jared Rathbone, entered the small sitting-room to which I had been escorted. He was a bear of a man, with bushy side whiskers which nearly obscured his face. He apologized for the delay and explained that the recent demise of Rudolph, the Crown Prince of Austria, had somewhat discommoded his usually efficient staff. Several of my fellow countrymen, it seemed, had substantial interests in Austria and were concerned lest any unrest cause by this unfortunate turn of events jeopardize their holdings.

"Ah, yes," I began, "the Fate of Princes touches all men." I prepared to offer several examples from antiquity, but the Consul pleaded urgent dispatches which required his attention.

"Now, how may I be of service, sir?"

"My teeth!" I exclaimed and raised my upper lip to illustrate. He quickly scribbled a name and address. "A fellow American," he assured me, "one of the very best in Europe. The late Louis Napoleon had old Evans as his personal dentist." I expressed my thanks and observed I had the utmost confidence in American skill. "You won't be disappointed," he added and left for his dispatches. Does not prophecy fill the very ether around us, had we but ears to hear?

Yet the prophecy was to tarry in its fulfillment. Thomas W. Evans, *dentiste*, of 2 rue Le Verrier, had still not returned from a week-end in the country. In broken English, a red-faced charwoman suggested that I come again, late tomorrow afternoon. Despondent, I made my way to my hotel where I spent a night which would have been torturous had it not been for the laudanum supplied by the porter's wife and for the distraction provided by a French tabloid.

With the aid of a dictionary, I spent several hours piecing together an account of Prince Rudolph's untimely death. The tragedy had occurred in, at, or around Mayerling, the imperial hunting lodge. The Prince and a party of close friends had been hunting bear deep in the Austrian forests. Only thirty-one years of age, the Prince had been cut down in his prime by an accidentally discharged bullet. Princess Stephanie, his wife, Emperor Franz Joseph and Empress Elisabeth, his parents—all Europe, in fact, grieved over so tragic a loss. His great personal promise, the hope of the Hapsburg Empire, the dream of a unified Europe—all snuffed out in an instant.

The visage of Rudolph stared at me from the cheap gray page. A magnificent hussar moustache floated above a firm, manly chin, below which could be seen the brass-buttoned jacket of an Austrian cavalry officer. But it was his eyes that haunted me. They seemed to protest so cruel a fate. There was also a photogravure of the Mayerling lodge, a dismal place, admirably suited to the imagination of a Mrs. Radcliffe. Turrets, towers, a baroque pavilion testified that death would be no stranger within its walls.

I awoke consumed by pain. Only through alternate doses of laudanum and brandy did I survive. But at last the hour arrived, and with my face swathed in flannel I set out for rue Le Verrier. It was Tuesday, the fifth of February, 1889, a day I have good cause to remember. Ah, the uses of adversity. How oft they reveal the gods steering our course.

The same charwoman greeted me and, seeing to my comfort in the treatment room, left me with assurances that the dentist would attend me shortly. I was aware that the room's appointments bespoke both taste and prosperity; that autographed photographic portraits and drawings, presumably of notables, adorned the walls. Yet my eyes continuously returned to the necessities of Evans' occupation. The treatment chair was centered in the room, and over it hung a chandelier which could be raised and lowered by a cunning counterbalance. A pink marble lavatory stood at hand, next to a table which held his instruments. I confess that the sight of the latter, in particular, gave me a quease.

The door opened and the dentist came toward me. I looked down into a pair of twinkling blue eyes. "Griswold, sir, Wilmot Rufus Griswold, a fellow American from the fair state of Maryland." I pumped his hand vigorously. He winced and backed away.

"Please be seated, sir," he said somewhat weakly. His thin neck and limbs coupled with a great corpulence about the middle reminded me of a well-fed robin, one very proud of his feathers. In fact, there was something disturbingly foppish about the man, but my teeth, my poor damaged teeth, distressed me so that I overcame all qualms and seated myself in his chair.

I briefly explained my problem. While he probed my teeth, I attempted when able to make conversation. "Your opinion, sir," I asked. "Does the new century begin on January first, 1900? Or—" Before I could proceed further, however, he placed a block of India rubber between my jaws. He resumed his probing, and finally informed me that I must lose two of my teeth.

"Definitely. For your relief, sir, I must remove two teeth." Allowing me no reply, he reached for a devilish-looking pair of pliers and poked them into my open orifice. I twisted and turned. When he touched a painful tooth, I am sorry to report, I screamed aloud.

The dentist withdrew a silk handkerchief from his smock and wiped perspiration from his forehead and upper lip.

"Berenice," he bawled, and the charwoman appeared with brandy and two glasses.

"Your health, sir," I said feebly. We drank. He topped my glass and I drank again. His soft fingers held my chin and he spoke quietly, soothingly, about our fair country. But as he again prepared to extract my bothersome teeth, he again brought that pair of devil's pliers into my view.

Terror overcame me. The next I knew, the poor fellow was waving his finger in the air. I had bitten him. He excused himself, cursing. Moments later, he returned with a bandage upon his finger and a tray bearing several bottles and a beaker. I stared in horror as he mixed salts and liquid.

"A simple nitrous compound," he explained and assured me that I would experience nothing untoward. He poured the solution over gauze. "Now simply inhale, Griswold, inhale very deeply." Reluctantly, I did as he bade and upon my third or fourth breath, I felt a great exhilaration.

"Remarkable," I observed and began to laugh. Evans insisted I breathe through the gauze again. "Gladly!" I fairly shouted. Indeed, so happy was my state, I was now reluctant to cease inhaling those delightful fumes. As if from a distance I heard my voice proclaiming the date upon which the new century would begin, recounting the virtues of noble Baltimore, and gaily discoursing upon the prospects of my business affairs. All the while, I was laughing.

Deftly, he blocked my jaws agape and raised his pliers. "Your tooth, sir," he said, waving it before my eyes. "And your other tooth," he announced with the air of a conjuror.

"Marvelous," I sighed, and closed my eyes.

She was there when I opened them—the most beautiful woman I had ever seen, hovering above me like some ethereal creature. "*Bonjour*," she said in a deep, husky voice. Never had I heard the French language sound so pure. "Hello," I answered, "hello, hello." Perfect lips turned upward in a smile and, as she tossed her head, gorgeous flamelike hair fell to her shoulders. Limpid brown eyes caressed me. She patted my cheek. "Hello," I repeated.

At her insistence, Evans introduced us. "Mr. Griswood, may I present Mademoiselle Laurent."

"Griswold," I corrected, "Wilmot Rufus Griswold at your service." She extended her hand, which I kissed fervently. "Mery," she said, "you must call me Mery." With an air of easy intimacy, she draped herself at full length upon a green and sable Turkish couch which filled the bay window. Her lineaments formed a graceful tableau which would have delighted any but the most modern of painters.

When I tried to speak again, Evans stuffed a large lump of cotton into my mouth. But I did not protest, for Mery chattered divinely—believe me, such is possible—of cafe society, of a new painter whose name I have forgotten, of a restaurant which had recently found favor among poets and artists. Mostly, however, she related the latest rumors surrounding the death of Prince Rudolph.

"Have you heard?" she asked. "It seems that poor Rudy was not shot but poisoned. And there was a young girl with him when he died, a girl who has since vanished most mysteriously."

Evans removed the cotton and I seized the opportunity to speak. Yet the influence of her heavenly presence, added to the euphoric effects of Evans' solution, prevented me from making the observations I intended. All I could utter was, "Marvellous, simply marvellous." The dentist roughly swabbed my bleeding gums.

"And what do you make of this, Thomas?" she continued. She read to us from a newspaper whose correspondent had learned from confidential and highly placed sources that Prince Rudolph had fought violently with his father and had deliberately snubbed the Emperor by failing to attend a family dinner on the very eve of his death. "How like Rudy," she added. Then, with great drama, she translated into English the paper's most startling claim: "Rudolph's death was not accidental. The Crown Prince was assassinated as a result of a plot involving the Emperor and Count Eduard Taaffe, the Austrian Premier."

"God save us from such nonsense," exploded Evans. "Why under heaven should old Franz Joseph kill his only son? He doted on him. Whenever we met, he was always insisting I look at Rudolph's teeth."

"According to *Le Gauloise*," answered Mery, "it was to prevent Rudy from accepting the crown of Hungary and thus fomenting a civil war within the Empire. Their correspondent contends that Rudolph had strong sympathies for the Hungarians and frequently was seen in the company of known revolutionaries. Fascinating, *n'est-ce pas?*"

"Fascinating," I sputtered, dislodging the cotton, which Evans immediately replaced. "Mr. Griswood will be leaving shortly," he then announced. Leave? When I had just met Mery Laurent? She came to my rescue. "Perhaps your countryman would care to join us at dinner," she offered most graciously. I nodded my head in vigorous assent.

"But it's Tuesday, *les mardistes!*" Evans cried. Yet Mery was not to be dissuaded, and to my joy I accompanied them to a cafe—the *deux* something or other—for an evening repast. My joy was short-lived, however, for Mery was on most cordial terms with the other patrons—entirely too cordial, I reflected, considering they were a most Bohemian group. She ignored me, while she bantered with them, several of whom took liberties with her. Further, the food was overly spiced, especially with garlic. Typically French.

Not wishing to appear unworldly, I ordered a second bottle of wine and toasted the beauty of women everywhere, especially our present companion. I observed how fortunate I was to reside in a state named for one Mary and, on foreign shores, to find myself in the blessed company of another. "But I am M-*e*-r-y," she informed me, stressing the vowel. A whim of her parents, I supposed to myself, forbearing any comment on yet another illustration of French perversity. Besides, the charming creature asked my reasons for visiting Paris. I told her of the approaching Exposition, of how I intended to make the fruits of American genius available not only to France, but to the world! Warming to my subject, I described the magnificent structure known as The Griswold Medical Dispensary, on Frederick Street, in Baltimore, in the state of Maryland. "My father, Robert Griswold, through unflagging devotion and ingenuity, discovered a tonic called, modestly enough, Bob's Oil. It grows hair," I said proudly. "If used in time, Bob's Oil will stop hair falling out, remove dandruff and restore faded hair to its natural color! The Griswold Medical Dispensary employs scores, hundreds even, of travelling men, many with their own wagons, who tour our great country to bring the benefits of Bob's Oil to all our citizens, even on the Western frontier."

From my pocket purse, I withdrew a *reclame*, as the French

call it, and showed it to her. The drawing depicted a gentleman before and after using but one bottle of Bob's Oil, his
gleaming pate later covered with a full growth of hair.

Mery pulled a strand of her flaming hair across her smiling
lips. "Should I become *denude*, Monsieur Gaudissart, I shall
remember." "Griswold," I hastened to correct her, and
promised to send a sample bottle to her for use, perhaps,
by an unfortunate relative.

Evans interrupted at this juncture by noisily clearing his
throat. He produced a massive gold watch with a damascened
cover and abruptly announced that it was time. "The *mardistes*
will be waiting," he insisted, as I vainly attempted to stay them
for another bottle of wine. From Mery's comments I divined
that they were to attend a *soiree*, and I suggested that I might
be welcome at such an affair.

Tenderly patting my hand, Mery became solicitous of my
health. I assured her that my jaw was in quite good order, to
which she agreed with a nod. Nevertheless, she explained,
this was more in the way of a *salon*, a gathering of devotees
of the arts, especially poetry. Undoubtedly, I would be bored.

"Heaven forbid," I exclaimed, "that you think the muse
of poetry has neglected our American shores. Why, think of
Henry Timrod, John Tabb, Norman Pinney, Rufus Dawes,
Ebenezer Bailey. I myself have dipped my quill in the Hy-
perian Spring," I added, and began to recite one of my better
efforts praising the boundless benefits of a mother's true
love in forming the moral character of her charges. Before
I was finished with the first canto, however, they made their
apologies and left. I followed, having some difficulty with the
waiter who presented me with a surprisingly large *l'addition*. I
overtook them at the curb, and before further objections could
be raised, I hailed a passing four-wheeler and we were
launched across Paris to my first *salon*.

Disappointment began almost immediately we emerged
from our carriage. The street, rue de Rome, was drab and
deserted. Number eighty-nine was an undistinguished looking

maison de rapport, as the French insist upon calling an apartment building. In the vestibule we picked our way through a gaggle of children who were marching about with wooden swords, banging on pots, and singing a song about some girl named Suzette. The stairwell smelled strongly of cabbage. Climbing to the third floor, which the French perversely count as the second, we paused at the end of a dimly lit corridor. Upon the door was pinned a simple card, hand lettered: STEPHANE MALLARME.

Could this be a *salon?* I asked myself.

We were welcomed cordially by our host, especially Mery— again! Although she did not mind, I decided that there should be limits to cordiality, even for a Frenchman. Aside from speaking tolerable English, our host struck me as absurd. He resembled nothing so much as a satyr recently escaped from the pages of some ancient Bestiary: small stature; intense, gleaming eyes; white moustache and goatee; and fringes of flowing white hair from which wide, pointed ears seemed to hang like pendants. Baggy trousers, rumpled soft-bosomed shirt, string tie askew, all indicated a deplorable carelessness about his person. And of all things, he wore a plaid shawl, draped over his shoulders and extending nearly to his knees. I should add that many of the other guests were dressed in fashions even more *bizarre.* I was appalled.

Although comfortably fitted up for family usage, the room was so crowded that I was forced to sit upon the floor. It was also warm to the point of actual discomfort. A large china jar of tobacco was provided for the use of the guests, and already the air was heavy with noxious blue smoke. *Les Mardistes*—so named because they met on *Mardi,* Tuesday— seemed not to mind in the least. The only refreshment was a bowl of rum punch which I found tasty if not at all elegant. To add to my disappointment, Mery deserted me and flitted about the room exchanging embraces and the like. Finally she settled upon a divan, next to a very old man whom I took for a relative, perhaps M. Mallarme's father.

Ah! how our first impressions do deceive us!

But such disappointments are indeed trivial compared with what next transpired. Our host positioned himself near a tile stove at the far end of the room. He began to speak. All conversation ceased. The stillness was reminiscent of a cathedral filled with the breathless faithful, whose presence makes the silence more imperative than were the place deserted.

So! Rather than the sparkling wine of fabled *salon* conversation and wit, I was served but the dregs of a preachment. In French! I did recognize a *mot* now and again and determined at last that our host was speaking of poetry. M. Mallarme was advancing, apparently, some fanciful theory of his own concoction which—I translate him correctly—held that poets are truly *alive* only after they are finally *dead*. How very French, I mused, bored to exhaustion.

Nonetheless, I rallied to my duty as a guest and listened most respectfully for what seemed hours. At length, when our host paused to insert a cigarette into a modish holder he affected, I made bold to offer a comment upon those sentiments which are proper to poetry.

"The *Iliad* for war," I cried, "and the *Odyssey* for wandering, but where, pray, is the great epic of Commerce? Arms, agriculture, love, travel, adventure, all have had their ample offerings of song. Now who among you shall string the lyre in praise of Commerce?" I paused for effect and was aware of a polite, in fact, total silence. Mery's beautiful lips were parted in a most exquisite fashion. I continued. "All the feats whereof poetic rapture ever sang surely are to be matched by those which are daily displayed in the service of Commerce!"

At this the old gentleman sitting next to Mery actually laughed aloud! His gaiety infected others, and soon the entire room joined in a general rollick. I admit the absence of my two damaged teeth did cause my speech to slur, to be marred in fact by an unnatural escaping of air, so that in pronouncing some words I seemed to whistle. Still, such behavior evidenced a lack of breeding and gentility which would not be tolerated among the better class of Baltimore's citizenry!

With dignity, I arose. In an effort to compose my thoughts, I addressed the punch bowl. As M. Mallarme droned on and on, I slyly studied that ancient vulgarian who had laughed at me. His complexion presented a vivid contrast to his rumpled, demode black suit, for he was totally wan, nay! cadaverous. His thin lips were pallid, lifeless. But as our eyes met, they twisted into a smirk. His nose spoiled what must once have been a handsome profile, for it had been broken and ill-healed, and now strayed off toward his left cheek. He was beardless—unfortunately so, for he had a noticeably weak chin which signified a corresponding want of moral energy.

And what hair! The color and texture of white cornsilk. But this odd old fellow had suffered it to grow all unheeded, nearly reaching his shoulders. Gossamerlike, wild, his locks floated rather than fell about his face. This was the more noticeable as he possessed an inordinate expansion above the regions of the temple. All together his was a countenance not easily forgotten. Again, his eyes touched mine, holding them enthralled. A sadness, mingled with a disturbing sense of familiarity, overcame me, and again I favored the punch bowl.

Lost in my revery, I was abruptly aware that M. Mallarme was addressing me: "I said, 'Are you familiar with the name of Edgar Poe?' "

"I believe I have heard of him," I replied rather coldly. "An American versifier in the early part of this century, was he not?" Indeed, I was more than passingly familiar with that name, but lest another incident be precipitated, I chose to hold my tongue. M. Mallarme then spoke a poem he had written—a poem dedicated, he maintained, to the same Mr. Poe. In deference to my presence, he next recited a translation of his lines into English. But, English or French, his verses made little sense. Merely some twaddle about monuments falling from heaven and new words for some tribe somewhere. To my astonishment, however, his performance moved the rest of his audience to tears. There is no accounting for French tastes, I philosophized, and visited the punch bowl. I recall staring at the crystal cup I held, remarking to myself how poor a service it was. I determined to investigate the possibility of supplying from America an inexpensive set of crystal which would be within the means of most Frenchmen.

I can record here nothing of the next hours, for I fear the exertions and strains of the day took their toll and I slept. My next clear memory is of awakening and being firmly convinced I had descended to Tophet! My head throbbed while within my skull reverberated a screech as of all the damned souls in unison. A pair of burning eyes gazed maliciously into mine. Gleaming white fangs presented themselves just inches from my face. I screamed.

Wearing a sympathetic smile, the visage of M. Mallarme appeared above me and he lifted a huge black cat from my shoulder. "Lilith," he explained, stroking the blasted beast. "She was once the pet of a poet's mistress. To have her sit upon your shoulder is an encouraging portent for your literary aspirations." In the distance I heard the wailing of a train's whistle, apparently the sound which awakened me and which I mistook for the cries of sinners.

"Mery?" I called, gazing about, only to discover the room was otherwise empty.

"Perhaps *une finale*," said M. Mallarme, gesturing toward the punch bowl. I accepted his invitation, fortified myself with a final cup and prepared to depart. Suddenly, the cat leapt from M. Mallarme's arms and paced expectantly before a closed door. A petite woman emerged, dressed in somber mourning from veil to shoes. M. Mallarme hurried to retrieve the mischievous Lilith, who nuzzled the woman's skirts. She turned and spoke to a figure in the darkened doorway. It was the old man who had laughed at me.

"We carry no money," she said to him in a lilting English voice. "Perhaps these will realize enough for you to begin." She reached behind her black cloak and fumbled to unlock a heavy silver necklace.

"Permit me, madame," I offered and sprang to her assistance. Taking the clasp from her fingers, I loosened the ends quickly. Raising her veil, she smiled briefly at me. "We thank you," she said, and I observed that she was not so young as I had thought, although her bright dark eyes still told of an active inner life. She slid two rings from the necklace: silver they were and encrusted with a variety of precious stones. These she presented to the old man. To my surprise, I saw she had a dozen or more rings which she wore upon the necklace, but her fingers were bare. An awkward moment passed as she stood waiting, before I realized she wished me to refasten the clasp.

"We are most grateful." She smiled at all, and glided out into the night.

"A charming woman," I enthused, for her very presence had made a warm impression upon me. "A relative?" I inquired innocently. Our host ignored my question, and offering his apologies, commented brusquely upon the lateness of the hour. He gathered his cat once again and retreated to an inner room. Determined to learn the identity of so charming a woman, I repeated my question to my former tormentor. He answered: "She is a mother bereft of her only son, and she will find no peace in this earth until she learns why."

Imagine my amazement! For these enigmatic words were not only spoken in English, but in tones and accent so similar to my own as to be indistinguishable. He continued staring at the door through which she had vanished, casually tossing the rings to and fro in his hands.

Turning to me, he spoke without warning, accusingly: "Gaudissart. A strange name for an American."

"Griswold," I hastened to correct, "Wilmot R. Griswold of Baltimore, Maryland, 'that City Divine blessed by the

Heavens with paradisical clime.' " His jaw sagged open, and for an embarrassing span of time he regarded me closely, as though examining my skull beneath my skin. In a rasping whisper he repeated my name, "Griswold. I knew that name once."

Since his speech declared him to be a fellow countryman, I ventured to mention some of my literary accomplishments which might be familiar to American readers. "Well, sir," I began modestly, "my verses in the columns of *Leslie's Magazine* have attracted some favorable comment." He snorted rudely and drained the punch bowl. He proved to be familiar with the household, for in a trice he opened a chest, extracted a bottle, and poured a tumbler near full of some brown liquid. He raised the glass: "To your health, sir, and to departed enemies!" In one gulp the glass was empty. He filled it again.

As I struggled with my Kitchener, I made one more effort to be civil. "Perhaps you are remembering my uncle, Rufus Griswold," I suggested. "He gathered no small fame as editor of *Graham's*. But of course his crowning achievement was a magnificent biography of Edgar Allan Poe, the American versifier with whom M. Mallarme seems so taken. I have the pleasure to be named for my uncle and entertain hopes that my own literary efforts may yet bring honor to his memory."

Turning to bid farewell, I was struck by a sight which haunts me still. The old man's cheeks, his whole head, seemed to have swollen as if he were suddenly strucked by a dropsical condition. He attempted to speak, but speech was plainly beyond his capabilities. At last he said but one word, repeating it over and over again in a maniacal fashion: "Griswold, Griswold. Griswold!"

He had let fall the tumbler, so I quickly refilled it and offered the draught to the poor man. He drank greedily and then began to shake as if the palsy had overtaken him. By main force, I seated him in a lounge chair and covered him with M. Mallarme's shawl. His condition worsened, and he fell into a fit of derangement. His words were but barely coherent. From English, he lapsed into French, then moved into German. There were indistinct mutterings, I believe, in Greek and Latin as well. He employed such words and phrases as cause me to blush even in recollection and are most certainly unfit to be repeated for ears polite.

This, in short, was the drift of his ravings. He accused my uncle not only of falsifying his account of the unfortunate Mr. Poe's life, but of actually conniving in a plot to murder the poet as well. He continued at great length to berate my uncle Rufus, becoming almost Biblical in his curses. I prepared to depart in silence. I was a guest. I do share some republican sentiments with our French cousins. But he had gone too far. After all, I am a Griswold.

Before taking my leave, however, I did attempt to calm him and restore his reason. I pointed out that I myself was from Baltimore and quite familiar with the circumstances surrounding the sorrowful life and tragic death of Mr. Poe. This but enraged him further.

"Baltimore," he shouted. "Mob Town! Mob Town! And now I hear they are even considering giving the vote to the fairer sex." He turned upon me, "Have you no shame, sir?"

Discerning no connection between the late Mr. Poe and woman's suffrage, I assumed his mind had snapped. As I finished the drop of rum in my glass, he rambled on and on, painting in the most vile words an incoherent picture of Mr. Poe as the victim of sinister political forces. And my connection, Rufus W. Griswold, was among the most sinister.

Patience deserted me. I informed him that I had myself stood beside the grave of the unfortunate poet and shed a manly tear over the loss of such genius. "But the loss was due to his own frailties," I concluded, "his debauchery, his trafficking with dangerous drugs and alcohol. Certainly not to any political conspiracy. Why, it was almost as if the stricken soul had actually desired to end his own life."

"Lies. Lies," he chanted.

"Truth, sir! Bitter, perhaps, but the truth. Why, as a youth I sat in a lyceum audience and listened to the account of Edgar Allan Poe's last days, an account given by Dr. Moran, the very physician, sir, who attended him in his final hours. I, the whole audience, had been swept along with pity and sorrow for the poor dissolute poet, driven to madness by drink, seeking solace in opium, yet in the end repenting. A great and noble heart at last made peace with his Maker."

The old man seemed to calm. He slumped in his chair, eyes shut tight. I believed for a moment that he was asleep and took two cautious, quiet steps toward the door. Without opening his eyes, he spoke: "Does it not strike you as curious, Master Griswold, that Dr. J. J. Moran deserted a promising medical practice to take up the lecture stage?"

I stopped. It was indeed a simple, logical question, but one which had never occurred to me. Yet, once pondered, the explanation became obvious.

"Dr. Moran, sir, had a noble soul, a soul in which mundane matters of personal profit took second place to the common good. How many youths did his lecturing save from trodding the path of a man like Poe, from suffering the ignominy of a drunkard's funeral, whatever their genius? How many men did the doctor rescue from being the bane of wife and family? A disgrace to friends? Could you have been present, sir, and heard that pitiful description of the poet's last hours, his ravings, his pleas for mercy, his final conversion and the attendant peace which the poet found . . . why, sir, there was not a dry eye in the hall, not a bosom which failed to heave in sympathy with the agonies and sufferings of the late Mr. Poe."

"The audience approved of Dr. Moran's lecture?" he asked, opening one eye. He closed it again. "Good," he said, smiling. "It was one of my better efforts."

A moment lapsed before the import of his words was felt in my mind. "Yours?" I asked. He simply smiled, more to himself than to me, as though he were enjoying some private joke.

"Since only Dr. Moran was present in that hospital room," I said, belching rum, "you must possess awesome powers of imagination to have written so vivid an account."

He opened both eyes. "You forget, my good Griswold," he spat out, "there was one other person present."

"Really, sir? And who might he have been?"

"Edgar Allan Poe, you fool." He closed his eyes.

I took my leave, being none too careful about quietly closing the door. I had had my fill of French conceits.

CHAPTER

2

"What right," said I, "had the old gentleman to make any other gentleman jump? If he asks me to jump, I won't do it, that's flat, and I don't care who the devil he is."

WITH WORN SPIRITS I GREETED THE NEXT GRAY DAWN. I stared into the cheval glass, steadying myself by clutching its frame. Red-streaked eyes couched in a puffed, sallow pudding of a face stared back. To continue at this pace would be madness. Reformation or ruin were my only alternatives. Necessarily I pledged to bend my nose to the grindstone. But I could not grapple with the problems of international commerce without teeth! So, restored by several headache draughts, I set off at once to the rue Le Verrier.

"Emergency. *Aidez-moi!*" I fairly screamed at the charwoman. She nodded, stifled a yawn and led me into the treatment room where I toured Evans' portrait gallery as I waited. Astonished, I halted before a photograph of a lovely woman of indeterminate age, dressed in a flowing dark gown and a voluminous feathered hat. It was the very woman I had met last evening at the *salon* of M. Mallarme. The signature read simply: *Elisabeth.*

"Oh, it's you," said Evans in a belligerent manner. "What's the emergency?" he asked struggling with a pair of galluses, awkwardly twisting them over his shoulders.

"Good morning, sir," I said with a heartiness I did not feel. "I wish you to fashion two artificial teeth as soon as possible. My business demands—"

"For God's sake, Griswood, after breakfast." Waving me to accompany him, he repaired to a sitting room where, in silence, he finished his coffee and devoured several of those horn-shaped pastries. I sipped the tepid milky coffee and finally spoke. "That woman in the photograph on your wall. Signed *'Elisabeth.'* She seems familiar. Might I inquire who she is?"

Brushing crumbs from his yet unshaven chin he answered gruffly. "Of course she seems familiar. That is Her Majesty, Elisabeth, Empress of Austria."

"Indeed, sir," I exclaimed and recounted my experience of last night. "I would swear it was the same woman, talking privately with the ancient humorist."

"Elisabeth? Here in Paris? That would be odd. Yesterday was her son Rudolph's funeral. A terrible tragedy that. Closeted with Le Rennet? I wonder . . ." He fell to contemplation.

"Is the ancient a relative of the Mallarmes?"

"What? Le Rennet? No, no. Although at times Stephane coddles him like a much-loved father. The man is a *fantast.* Claims to be Edgar Allan Poe. He has become a *monstre sacre* among a small group of literati. Not that he hasn't a way with words, and an exceptionally keen mind."

An hour later I was seated in *that* chair, a slop jar in my arms, and my teeth clamped on some waxy material. The charwoman announced she was leaving to do her marketing. Within seconds she returned, screaming *"Poivrot! Poivrot!"*

41

Drunkard! I had early acquired the meaning of the word from my hotel porter.

A commotion ensued and the woman and Evans returned, half-carrying, half-dragging between them the ancient Le Rennet, obviously drunk to the high heavens. I spat out the wax and made bold to offer a sentiment upon drunkenness. I was ignored. They placed the sot upon the couch and Evans sent the woman on an errand as he himself raced from the room. I arose and studied the frail figure reclining on the couch. His breathing was short, broken. His skin was ghostly pale and his noble forehead was heavily beaded with perspiration. His withered face wore an expression of anguish or perhaps even terror.

"His heart has failed, fool!" said Evans, rudely pushing me aside. He administered a hypodermic to the unconscious man, then threw his head on the heaving chest and listened intently. Ripping open the old one's shirt, he next applied a blister directly over the heart. Finally the dentist covered him with a blanket, solicitously wiping the wrinkled brow. I returned to the chair and waited.

In barely a quarter-hour the charwoman returned, accompanied by a gaunt youth dressed in a black frock coat and brandishing a stethoscope. After consulting briefly with Evans, he began a systematic examination of the elderly patient. At length, satisfied, he mumbled some instructions to the dentist and left—whistling loudly.

"He'll live, though God knows how," Evans said, addressing the wall, not me. "I wonder what he was coming to see me for?" Remembering that I was present, Evans sighed and suggested I return in the afternoon.

Disappointed and still somewhat indisposed, I retired to a cafe. Smoke and the odor of sour wine upset me further so I ordered a medicinal brandy. Uninvited, a Frenchman sat down in the chair opposite me babbling all the while, seeking my opinion, I at last deduced, upon the mysterious death of

Prince Rudolph. I attempted to inform him that I was unaware of any mystery, but my French was not equal to the task. After one more brandy, I left, my mind teased by another mystery: who was old Le Rennet?

"Oh, it's you," said Consul Rathbone when at length I was escorted into his office. He did not even rise.

"Good morning, sir," I offered cheerily.

"Aha! You have been to Evans!"

"Indeed I have," I said, aware once again of the slight whistling sound as I spoke. "A fine example of American skill in the healing arts. Our country can be proud—"

"Well, well?" he interrupted.

"Perchance I have met an elderly gentleman. By his accent and speech, a fellow American. In fact, he claims to hail from my own part of our fair land."

"Yes," he fairly growled.

"Well, sir, this Le Rennet—"

"Henri Le Rennet!" the Consul thundered.

"Yes, I believe that may be his name."

"And he claims to be Edgar Allan Poe?"

"He does imply some such thing," I responded, surprised to learn that Rathbone was familiar with the subject of my inquiry.

"How much money did you give him?" he demanded, simultaneously banging his fists upon his massive desk and rising out of his chair.

"But I gave him no money."

"Thank God for that. Some of your countrymen have not been so fortunate." He fell back into his chair. "Last year I had a man in here. Angry as a wet hen. Couldn't blame him. His wife had given Le Rennet over five hundred dollars. Claimed the scoundrel helped her write some poesy. Drivel! It made no sense at all. Felt sorry for the fellow, but I couldn't help him. And the police wouldn't. No crime had been committed, so why should they care? Since then I've heard that

Le Rennet is thick as thieves with them."

"The man is a proven fraud, then?"

"Of course! A hoaxer. These fellows play upon the extravagant gullibility of the age. They set their wits to work in the imagination of schemes to hoax impressionable intellects. Despicable. The more so because they all too often succeed." He stared into the air, rubbed his nose, meditating. "The world is full of such people." Reaching into a japanned box which stood beside his desk, he rummaged a moment, muttering, then withdrew a crumpled paper and spread it on the desk before me. On it was written in a bold hand:

RUDOLPH—S.S.PARRAMATTA—DEGROTE—VICOMTE
DE MONTREINE

"You see? This is the sort of thing I have to contend with." The Consul had surely warmed to his subject, but his point was far from clear. I said as much. "Two days ago. Monday. Right before I was to leave for dinner. Ruined my appetite. This farmer from Kansas demanded to see me. A fine, staunch American and a prohibitionist to boot. He brings me this story of a priest he had met while journeying in Italy. This priest, Degrote—it's all there—this priest claims to have been travelling aboard some British steamship where he met a French count—certainly, by all means, a count—who informed him of Prince Rudolph's death."

I smiled and said nothing. Rathbone, however, seemed to think a reply was in order. "Don't you see, this priest was on the high seas and was informed of Rudolph's death on the afternoon of the twenty-ninth of January."

"Yes." I continued to smile, thinking I should humor the man.

"Rudolph wasn't dead until the next morning, the thirtieth! Now do you see? Hoaxers. Wretched concoctors of contemptible falsehoods." He arose. "Be warned. Good day to you, sir." He marched out, and I, unawares, placed the scrap of paper in my pocket. Ah, truly, there is no armor against Fate.

Contemplating the Consul's words, I made a midday meal of some sticky melted cheese which the cafe owner assured me was the pinnacle of French cuisine. A bottle of wine was required to wash it from between my teeth. I returned to rue Le Verrier and was admitted by the charwoman who was just leaving. As I made my way toward the treatment room, I hesitated, suddenly aware of voices from a different chamber. One of them belonged to the bewitching Mery Laurent.

"But, Thomas, you must help poor Henri." I again reflected upon the magical charm of Mery's voice. "He needs you desperately." None but a cad could refuse her.

"Why me?" rejoined the dentist. "There will be the devil's own confusion if I go." I had nearly resolved to oblige Mery myself when I was startled by Le Rennet's entering the discussion.

"Because you will have access to her presence. As her dentist, you can come and go without arousing much suspicion from Taaffe and his men. You can ask polite questions. You can be my eyes and ears in the Hofburg. She expects you." His voice was surprisingly strong, although his speech was slightly slurred.

"But I will have to close my doors, let my patients suffer. And the expense! And all for what? Because you have promised Elisabeth the impossible? Taken advantage of that dear woman in her grief? What can you hope to accomplish that the combined efforts of the entire Austro-Hungarian Empire cannot? And why are you so distrustful of Count Taaffe? Fine fellow. He and Rudolph didn't always get along, but that means nothing. Anyway, it's over now."

"No. It will not be over until I learn the truth of what happened to Prince Rudolph and the young girl."

"But look what you are asking of me. To disrupt my life, just to be part of this . . . this . . ." Words failed the dentist.

45

"Thomas, you know Henri has been helpful in the past. Even Etienne has said as much, hmmmm?" I lingered on that last syllable.

Le Rennet spoke accusingly. "I seem to remember an English girl and her brothers and some nonsense about a New Zealand gold mining stock. As I recall, I solved that little puzzle to your satisfaction—and profit!"

Evans muttered a string of indistinguishable words. "Mery, if this is so important, then surely you should accompany me."

"But who will take care of Henri? Besides, the court will be in mourning, Vienna will be so dull."

I was about to announce my presence when the dentist stormed past me and out the front entrance.

"But what of my teeth?" I called.

"Damn your teeth, sir," he replied and slammed the door.

"Why, it is the illustrious Gaudissart," sang Mery Laurent. Having accustomed myself to the French habit of calling friends by familiar names, I merely bowed and tenderly raised her outstretched hand to my lips. "Come, come, you must say *hallo* to poor Henri," and I followed her, more from a desire to remain in her divine presence than to visit the ancient invalid. "Henri, it is your countryman."

I found him a parody of an Eastern potentate. He sat in a huge bed, propped and bolstered on all sides by pillows, a gold-threaded blanket wrapped about his shoulders, and a flannel night-cap askew upon his head. He glared at me imperiously. Color had returned to his cheeks, his breathing was regular. His manner was as irascible as on the previous evening. He acknowledged my presence with a grunt, draining a glass of wine at the same time. In short, he showed but scant sign of having so recently escaped the Grim Reaper.

"I am pleased to witness your recovery, sir," I began and, recalling Mery's solicitude toward him, I proffered my assistance. He laughed uproariously and was justly rewarded with a fit of coughing.

"But he might be of some service," Mery said, removing my

46

chapeau and playfully running a finger through my hair.

"Like his damned uncle Rufus served me?" Le Rennet snarled. Since he had been so recently near death I took no offense at his slur against the good name of Griswold, nor did I accost him with what I had learned at the Consulate.

Mery sprang to my defense. "Ah, but you must let him help you. Perhaps he could be your *brosseur*, eh?" I grew alarmed as I had no idea what a *brosseur* might be—only later did I deduce that it was some office of factotum or valet. Le Rennet's eyes grew dreamy. "Monsieur Brosseur. I like the sound of that. Yes. Monsieur Brosseur. Monsieur Brosseur." He repeated the words as though he were in a trance, and the way his lips seemed to mold themselves around the syllables, why it was almost as if he were *tasting* them. "Yes, I could do something with that. Or at least once I could have. Bah!" With a trembling hand, he refilled his glass. "So, Master Griswold, you wish to assist me in my investigations? Perhaps you also wish to undo some of the damage done me by your uncle?" He glowered.

"I wish only to get my teeth repaired," I replied, having no idea what sort of embarrassment, if not danger, the so-called investigations of a mad old man might place me in.

Mery spoke and her voice seemed to waft over me like perfume. "But think of poor Elisabeth, a mother deprived of her only son who was sent to his grave before his time. Still she does not know what has occurred. She worries. She fears. She has bad dreams. She cannot sleep. And only Henri—"

With forgivable impatience I interrupted her. "Am I to believe that the Empress of Austria has actually engaged this—"

"And just what did that old bungling humbug Rathbone tell you about me?" Le Rennet demanded.

"That you were a fraud, sir," I cried, "a damnable hoaxer who plays upon the gullible with some crude invention that you are Edgar Allan Poe. Why, any pitiable member of that loathsome tribe of penny-a-liners would be shamed by such a tale." I stopped abruptly, recalling that I had said absolutely nothing of my visit to the Consulate.

Apparently noting my confusion, Le Rennet grinned wickedly at me, then began a rolling chuckle which ended in more laughter and yet another fit of coughing.

"Well?" he asked in grandiloquent tone.

"A most fortunate guess, sir."

"Bah! Master Griswold, you wear a window in your breast, like most men. You can conceal nothing from me."

"Surely an extravagant claim, sir. A lucky guess and nothing else allowed you to divine my errand."

"Nonsense. I am not in the least extravagant, merely a skilled practitioner of ratiocination. Consider. Evans mentioned that the American Consul referred you to him. This is a common practice of Rathbone's as Evans is the only resident American dentist in Paris."

"But that was yesterday."

"And today, you say you are pleased with my recovery, so quite obviously you were here earlier. Most probably told to return this afternoon to have Evans fashion your teeth. Certainly you did not return to see old Le Rennet, eh? You are not of a nature to simply wander the streets of Paris, nor would the galleries, museums, bookstalls, or cafe society interest you. You lunched rather badly, as a spot on your cravat shows, and since you did not change your linen, you have evidently not returned to your hotel. So how did you otherwise fill the last hours? Upon your coat and your trouser's cuff, look!"

I looked and could see nothing but a few pine needles which I brushed away.

"They are Loblolly needles, Griswold. The trees are native to our fair South. I remember them well in Maryland. Do you not? In a misguided display of patriotism, the previous Consul shipped a dozen Loblollies to Rathbone. They are dying in this clime, forever shedding their browned needles.

They line the walks to the Consulate steps. *Ergo,* you have been to the Consulate."

I smiled and made some witticism about Le Rennet's reputation as a *charlataneris* being well-deserved. "Fool. When you offered to assist me, your hand moved unerringly to your wallet. Why, sir? Money was obviously on your mind and who but Rathbone would have put thought of my financial condition into your hollow skull? You are an open book, Master Griswold. And a boring volume to boot." He dismissed me with an imperious wave of his hand and closed his eyes.

"Your skills in deducing the obvious are of little interest to me," I replied, stung by his remarks. "But, if you must know, I did visit the American Consulate today."

"You were driven there, Master Griswold, to learn more about old Le Rennet. Admit it."

"And I was warned about you! Hoaxers are an all-too-common breed, sir." I rehearsed the tale which Rathbone had recited about the priest Degrote and his mad story of being informed of Rudolph's death while the Prince was apparently still alive.

Le Rennet's mien of insolent lethargy vanished and he seemed to exude an aura of animal-like cunning. "Do you still have that paper?" he demanded.

"I do, and if you collect such examples of hoaxes you are welcome to it."

A gnarled, age-spotted hand darted and pulled the paper from my grasp. "So. So," he repeated, gazing at it. "Get my clothing, Griswold. I must visit Etienne immediately."

"But, Henri," began Mery, but Le Rennet was not to be deterred. "Make me some broth. I shall be fine. Hurry." With difficulty I assisted the old man into his clothes, which now included a shirt of Evans'. Later I accompanied him to the street and hailed a hack.

"*Prefecture de police,*" he ordered the surprised driver. Turning, he stared intently at me. "Yes, a dull book. But still a line or two of the text might prove useful. Dinner this evening, nine o'clock. At *La Vie de Patachon*. Mery will accompany you." And he sped away.

The prospect of an evening in the company of Mery Laurent cheered me. When Mery greeted the suggestion with equal enthusiasm, my spirits soared.

"So it is decided," she bubbled. "You will help Henri."

"What?"

"You will assist poor Henri, of course."

"But my dear Mery," I pleaded, grasping her hands in my own. "I can do no such thing. I have my affairs to attend to, my business obligations. The demands of commerce are great and progress cannot be impeded by personal whim." I was firm. She pouted and poured two glasses of wine.

"Think of the opportunity. You can aid Henri in unravelling the Mayerling *affaire*. It is most important. It is unparalleled. You will go down in history!" I remained adamant. She refilled my glass. "We could work with Henri to-geth-er." She drew out the last word. The music of it hung in the air. I succumbed, suggesting that I might arrange an hour or two at some mutually convenient time. "But no! Henri needs someone constantly by his side."

I sighed, and tried to explain. "Business is business," I observed sternly. "Time is money. Work precedes pleasure. Moreover, what can old Le Rennet hope to discover? An invalid, in Paris, attempting to pierce the curtain of a supposed mystery which occurred hundreds of miles away?"

"But Henri has his methods."

"Pure harumphery," I stoutly maintained. "He will find nothing."

I refilled our glasses. "To you, Mademoiselle," I toasted, hoping to turn the conversation. She was silent for some moments.

"Would Monsieur *faire une gageure*?"

"Pardon?"

"How do you say, 'make a wager'?"

Happily intrigued, I nonetheless informed her that a gentleman would never gamble money with a member of the fair sex. "Something else, then? You will help poor Henri, and if he does not resolve the *affaire* at Mayerling, then perhaps Monsieur Griswold would care to take a week in the country at Valvins. We could go together." Together. That word again. I gazed into her brown eyes, limpid pools into which I might gladly throw myself. "We could travel as man and wife," she added huskily. She sipped from her glass, her lips caressing the vessel. Only then did the import of her words, the terms of her wager become clear. It was the most *bizarre* idea I had ever heard of. But in my weakened state, I am ashamed to admit, I accepted her challenge without hesitation. I seated myself beside her on the divan and with a trembling hand refilled our glasses.

"Done," I said, almost choking, as I raised my glass to seal our bargain.

"Get up, Griswood, I need your help." I must have dozed. Evans loomed in the doorway, Gladstone in hand, pointing to a trunk at his feet.

"But my teeth!" I exclaimed, confused and startled by his presence.

"Here, take these." He handed me a packet of toothache wax, tooth soap, and a bristle brush. He lectured me sternly on brushing my teeth twice each day. And also on avoiding familiarity with Mademoiselle Laurent.

"Mery," he shouted. "I am booked on the Express and it leaves in just forty minutes. Can't you hurry?"

She appeared, radiant, in an evening dress of green satin and feathers. "*En route!* And do not worry about me, Thomas. I shall keep busy."

"No doubt," growled Evans, and cast a sharp look in my direction. They left and I struggled with the trunk, but soon we were all in a four-wheeler recklessly careening through the streets. We arrived at the station with but minutes to spare. Despite Evans' hurried protest, Mery did not leave our coach, and I greeted the dentist's departure into the throng of travellers with relief. "And now to Henri," Mery said, leaning her head upon my shoulder. All thoughts of Evans vanished before we had rounded the next corner.

The cafe was disappointing in the extreme. It was located in a rundown riverfront neighborhood and I could not understand the presence of several rather luxurious carriages drawn up before its doors. The interior was dark as a tomb. "It's restful, Master Griswold, and quite discreet," said Le Rennet, as Mery unerringly found his table, myself stumbling behind. Another gentleman was with him, and he arose to bend politely over Mery's hand.

Le Rennet performed the introductions. "Master Griswold, may I present Alexandre Etienne, Prefect of the Paris Police." The Prefect smartly touched two fingers to a forelock and said, in passable English, "At your service, sir."

When seated, I studied the man as best I could by the flickering candlelight. His appearance was obviously military, even though he was dressed in mufti. He was tall and possessed a certain daredevil expression, emphasized, perhaps, by his flamboyant mustachio. Nevertheless, his immaculate grooming bespoke a man of significance, one who takes time at his toilet from both personal and public pride. I cannot deny I was surprised that such a respectable personage should be taken in by a sham like old Le Rennet. But taken he was. Their conversation, though guarded, was animated, punctuated on his part with those French gesticulations which seem to endanger all the crystal in the vicinity. Their language, too, was French, rapid and virtually unintelligible. I sipped my wine, gazing at Mery through the pulsing light of the candles.

"You see, Henri was right!" she cried, startling me. I confessed that I did not see or understand at all. "But it is simple. Thomas was followed onto the train by one of Taaffe's secret police who masquerades as a *functionaire* at the Austrian Embassy. Etienne has one of his best men on the train also. They follow Thomas, and we follow them. It is simple, *n'est-ce pas?*"

"But why," I inquired, "should a member of the Austrian police follow a dentist from Paris to Vienna?"

"If we were certain of the answer to that question, Master Griswold, Thomas would not have journeyed to Vienna and you would possess two new teeth."

When the waiter brought our dinner, Etienne rose and, pleading official duties, made his *adieus.* Yet before leaving he spoke softly to Le Rennet, in English. "Be careful, Monsieur. You are in deep waters." Troubled, I watched his powerful frame recede, then turned to my dinner. I dawdled, the events of the past few hours having robbed my appetite. I was but half finished when Le Rennet interrupted my thoughts.

"It is time to go home, Griswold."

"Home" I repeated to myself as I escorted Mery from the restaurant. "Home." The very word seemed to reverberate within me, and as we rode across the Seine and drove down the glittering Boulevard St. Germain, I recited for the benefit of my companions the attractions of my own fair Baltimore. My sentiments seemed to sadden Le Rennet, and I sought to restore his spirits. "Sir, if you are a fellow American, as I believe you to be, then surely you could travel once again to our native shores."

He was silent for so great a length, that I was convinced he had not heard my words. Then, suddenly, he spoke: "Home. Yes, now that all has been forgiven, or at least forgotten, I suppose I could go home. But perhaps it would be better if I remained here. Dead. After all, Master Griswold, where is home?" As if to underscore his words, the hack veered off into one of those damnable twisting streets and came to rest before an immense, time-eaten and grotesque mansion which stood tottering to its fall at the end of a short nameless lane. The sight was truly appalling. I attempted a light remark to bolster Mery's spirits, but she was not the least affected by the stagnant gloom which surrounded the place. Rather the opposite. Taking my arm, she led me into a large ground floor room, lit a lamp, and exclaimed, *"Magnifique!"*

Hardly the word I would have chosen. I picked my way through a clutter of tattered furnishings. Glumly I placed kindling and scraps in the gigantic fireplace to furnish more illumination as well as ward off the cold which seemed to ooze from the bare stone walls. As the flames grew higher, I noted that the grimy window panes were fitted with shroudlike drapery which would submerge the room in near total darkness at a blazing noon. My eyes could not reach the remoter angles of this chamber nor the recesses of the vaulted ceiling. A fitting home indeed for old Le Rennet.

Apparently oblivious to his surroundings, Le Rennet happily played host. More lamps were brought and he prepared quantities of an excellent rum flip which I drank thirstily. It was warming as well as delicious. "Old Benny Havens' secret recipe," said the ancient, but when I asked who Mr. Havens was, Le Rennet stared into the blazing fire as if it were a long corridor of years. "I was at West Point," he said finally, not taking his eyes from the fire. "Benny Havens and his wife conducted a tavern there. Benny was the sole congenial soul in the entire Godforsaken place." The old man raised his glass in a silent salute and lapsed into a revery or sleep, I could not tell which.

I took the opportunity to move closer to Mery. "Supposing there really is a mystery about Prince Rudolph's death—what might my contribution be to solving it? Am I to sleuth people? Or scurry about the streets of Paris searching out clews to a hunting accident at Mayerling? An accident witnessed apparently by several reliable personages?"

"You are being tedious." Le Rennet spoke without opening his eyes. "There are but three witnesses. His valet, Johann Loschek. And two companions who were invited to Mayerling for a hunt on that particular day: Count Joseph Hoyos and Prince Philip of Coburg, both of whom were present when the bodies were discovered."

"Bodies?" I exclaimed.

"But of course," said Mery. "There was a young girl with him. She also is said to have killed herself." Mery's beautiful brown eyes were sparkling with excitement. "Rudy was supposed to have been madly in love with her. What was her name?"

"Vetsera, Baroness Mary Vetsera," said the somnambulant Le Rennet.

"That's it. But he was married, and she was not of the royalty. Their cause was hopeless, so they died together rather than live apart."

"Persiflage," exploded Le Rennet, opening his eyes.

Naturally I sprang to Mery's defense. "But even in Baltimore such things have been known to happen. Who is immune to the darts of Venus?"

"Cupid, Griswold. Cupid's darts. But never mind that. What is of interest is the new version of Rudolph's last hours which the Austrian government has issued. Suicide. Bah!"

"Suicide?" I asked.

"The new fiction proceeds thus: Rudolph was depressed. Rudolph drank a bit. Rudolph became deranged. In said fit of derangement, he killed himself. But since he was not in command of his senses, he was technically not a suicide. Hence, yesterday the fifth of February at four-thirty in the afternoon, Crown Prince Rudolph was laid to rest with the Church's blessing and a state funeral."

"And this Vetsera woman?" I asked.

"Her presence at Mayerling is known, but has yet to be officially acknowledged. She is also known to be dead and buried. Presumably a double suicide." Le Rennet's skepticism was quite evident in his voice.

"Surely you must admit such an explanation is possible?"

"Our first task is to separate the merely possible from the probable. In probable events, when we have verified sufficient of them, we shall discern a pattern. A design forms. For many, this inherent design is called 'truth.' Its discovery is our goal."

I again inquired of my part in discovering this grand design. "You will help," Mery said. And after much questioning I discovered that I was to be an errand boy. Also I was to help Le Rennet with his correspondence, since his hands were frequently arthritic. Moreover, though his vision was surprisingly good, his eyes often suffered when strained. So I would read aloud some mysterious documents to him. Then, with Mery's help, I would supervise his diet, of especial importance given his seizure this morning. And, finally, I was to attempt restraining his intemperate habits.

I drew her aside. "My dearest Mery," I pleaded, "I might as well move in with the old scoundrel."

"Aha! Marvelous." Gaily she bussed me on the cheek and called across the room. "Henri. Wilmot has a marvelous idea. He will become your lodger and stay with you always. Is that not grand?"

"It is not grand at all," I protested, but Le Rennet prepared yet more flip, and Mery chattered divinely of Paris, and the night wore on. Further objections were hopeless, and some time near dawn we toasted my arrival at my new home.

I awakened upon the floor covered by a rug, my feet reposing upon a small overthrown table, amid the fragments of a broken glass intermingled with newspapers. A window had been flung open and the sun scalded my eyes. I felt I must be dying.

"Drink this," old Le Rennet said in a not unkind tone. Stooping at painful expense to his age-stiffened joints, he proffered me a glass of horrid red mush. Tomato pulp, my nose told me. And worse. It was topped with rum!

"Impossible," I swore. "I would not touch that concoction with a pair of tongs!" He insisted. I drank. Odd to say, after my second glass, my stomach was restored and my spirits rose.

"You might purchase more rum on your return from your hotel," he said, and I groaned as recollections of last evening flooded over me. I had forgotten but not Le Rennet. My work as a *brosseur* had begun.

CHAPTER

3

By a route obscure and lonely,
Haunted by ill angels only . . .

MORE RUM INDEED! WHAT NEED HAD I NOW OF RUM? WHILE resident in that dank, gloomy manse, my soberest moments rivaled those of the rankest swillbelly. Deliriums? I was companion to a mad old man who was either a genius or the most unprincipled hoaxer of our age—I do not know which, and at times I entertain both opinions of his character simultaneously. Delusion? I was witness to the unravelling of the most ingenious crime in recent history—but I cannot be certain that this crime had actually been perpetrated. Horrors? Arrested by the *gendarmerie,* I was cast into a dungeon and gnawed upon by rats. The merely *bizarre?* I was present while a presumably learned and respected physician described in disgusting detail the most perverse sexual practices ever heard by civilized man, and then I was asked to believe that such doings were common to our times.

And always, there was the intoxicating Mery Laurent.

An incident occurred the very morning of my removal which quickly caused me to repent my folly in quitting a comfortable hotel and taking lodgings with Le Rennet. Somehow I had to make a habitable space for myself in his decrepit manor. My search for a room was limited since I could not proceed beyond the ground floor. Both the main and rear staircases were broken and strewn with rubble. Moreover, although there were some dozen rooms upon the ground level, the majority were boarded up. The chamber I finally selected was large and lofty, with long, narrow pointed windows. Unfortunately, these were at so vast a distance from the blackened oak floor as to be altogether inaccessible from within. They were also filthy, admitting but little light. Still, the fireplace functioned and, most important, there was a key to fit the door's lock—the only room so provided. In my state of mind, I demanded the security, albeit scant, of a locked door.

With an inducement afforded by a considerable sum of money, the hotel porter and his strapping hulk of a son agreed to assist me with my baggage and attend to whatever scrubbing and the like would be necessary. However, as we were unloading my sample cases onto the house's steps, a group of street urchins began to pelt us with stones. After the porter's son chased them away, the surly hack driver I had engaged told us the building had once been a *maison de sante,* a madhouse, in which several grisly murders had occurred under mystifying circumstances.

Upon hearing this tale, the porter and his son crossed themselves several times in the Roman fashion and flatly refused to enter the building. Finally we agreed upon a sum which was three times the initial price, and my bags and sample cases were carried over the threshold and mops and brushes applied with hurried diligence. I sought out the old man, who verified the tale: the building had been a madhouse and had witnessed several murders; further, he asserted that because of some slight service he had performed for the physician who had operated the home, he was allowed to reside there for the remainder of his life, at a modest annual payment.

We were interrupted by the appearance of the porter, who demanded my presence immediately. I returned with him, to discover his son pointing at the closet, a look of terror upon his face. "The wall moves," said the porter. There was indeed a crack of some six inches between the rear and side walls of the closet. We pushed in unison, and with a screeching and clanging as if from all the engines of hell, the wall swung aside to reveal a black hole. Gathering my courage, I lit a lamp and, leading the pair, returned to the closet, determined to investigate. It was a totally unnerving sight. A room perhaps nine feet by fifteen feet. No windows and, it seemed, no air. Swatches of heavy batting, moldering, hung from the room's walls, to which manacles were also bolted. Chains lay in serpentine patterns on the stone floor.

"My God," I exclaimed, and ran down the corridor shouting for Le Rennet.

He was unperturbed. "Yes, that's what I knew must have happened. But those poor souls have long since fled, Griswold, and are better forgotten." We re-entered the room and ordered the closet boarded shut. The remainder of the job was completed with more haste and little diligence. The pair demanded their wages and rushed gratefully into the sunlight. In all honesty, I could not blame them. Discouraged, I fell onto a threadbare chair which belched dust in protest. I spied my sample cases across the room. The name BOB'S OIL emblazoned in crimson and gold upon each seemed to accuse me, to ask the very question which pulsed through my brain: just what in the world was I doing here? As if in answer, Le Rennet entered, greatly agitated. "You must go to the telegrapher's office. With a message for Evans. Dispatch it to him at the Hofburg."

"What is the Hofburg?" I asked, feeling foolish when he guffawed a response. "It is the official residence of the Emperor of Austria. It is magnificent. You should visit it sometime."

"And what is the urgent message?" I asked, miffed.

"Here," he said, handing me a carefully lined slip of paper. On it was lettered:

WZYRSRNPLZBFNRTZPEKG

"But what does it mean?" I demanded, fearing some joke. "It means," said Le Rennet in that imperious tone he used when he considered a question beneath him, "it means that you will have to ask the telegrapher to repeat the message twice to be absolutely certain that it is dispatched precisely as it is written."

When I returned, he was gone. As the hours passed, I became alarmed. Recalling my promise to Mery that I would care for him, as well as succumbing to the lonely gloom that house created in me, I set out to effect his rescue. Carefully I picked my path through those twisting streets, trying to remember each turn faithfully so that I could find my way back again. Futile. Within the half-hour I was lost. But Fortune did not desert me entirely. In a modest cafe—the eleventh I had scouted—I discovered Le Rennet.

The old wanderer was sitting quietly by himself in a corner, and offered no explanation of his activities. With relief I noted that the markers on the table indicated he had consumed but three glasses of wine, and that he seemed not the least inebriated. Impulsively I suggested we dine together at that very cafe. He cheerfully agreed, and removed a veritable cabbage head of bills from his pocket. They were all franc notes in surprisingly large denominations.

"Elisabeth's rings," he answered my surprised exclamation. "Her generosity befits her exalted station. We are now obligated, Master Griswold, and we must not disappoint her." He ordered a sumptuous plate of veal cooked in wine and mushrooms. But if I expected the evening's conversation to center upon the Mayerling *affaire,* I was to be disappointed. Le Rennet chose to expatiate upon his personal experiences.

I cannot pretend to recount all that he told me on that occasion—the first of three—but I learned that he unquestionably believed himself to be Edgar Allan Poe. Once or twice, upon my venturing to express incredulity in respect to his pretensions, he grew very angry indeed. At length I considered it the wiser policy to say little and let him have his way.

After another bottle of excellent wine, I began to fall in with his narrative. "If what you say is true, sir, then you must be impossibly old." I hiccupped largely.

"I was eighty last January. Stephane held a small private celebration. That was probably why the poem he dedicated to me was in his mind. 'To give a new meaning to the words of the tribe.' Yes, I did try, Griswold. And sometimes I think I succeeded."

I proposed a toast to poets of yesteryear, to the handmaidens of the Muse, *et cetera,* when I realized that Le Rennet had heard nothing I had said. He was intently studying a woman who was mopping slops from a nearby table. The ensuing scene—the nearly deserted room, the woman, Le Rennet—cannot be forgotten. As she wiped, the woman emptied the remaining few drops of liquor from each glass. When she had cleared away the dishes and silver from our table, old Le Rennet poured her a glass of wine. She drank it greedily in one gulp, and gathering the old man's head to her ample bosom, she crooned, *"Ahh, merci. Merci."*

"Is it Muddy, then?" he whispered, and, childlike, he seemed content to remain cradled in her large embrace. She resumed her circuit of tables and Le Rennet gruffly shouted for a brandy. I was disconcerted in the extreme to see the change which had occurred in his visage. If possible, he seemed to have aged. His lips twitched out of control. Tears welled in his eyes, and finally streamed down his creased cheeks. He made no attempt to hide his condition, nor offer any explanation save this.

"That was the damnedest part, Griswold. I couldn't tell Muddy. I couldn't even tell Muddy!"

I tried to calm his sudden desperation, inquiring who

Muddy might be. "My wife's mother," he replied. "And mine."

As his sorrow for this lost, apparently incestuous, relative increased, he screamed for more brandy. "To their damnation. Every one of them. And an especial corner of hell for Rufus Griswold." His sorrow had turned to spiteful anger and I am afraid that I responded in kind, not simply from his maligning my family but also from the work and worry he had caused me that day. If he heard my brute words, he gave no indication.

"And a good evening to you, sir. We shall not meet again."

Outside, I fastened my coat, donned my hat, and set off at a brisk pace, determined to sever all connections with Le Rennet. But by the time I had traversed a half-dozen or so of those streets, my pace slowed. I could not rid myself of Mery's beauty, of my promise and of hers. And, in the corner of my mind, so to speak, sat that wretched old man with tears streaming down his cheeks. I turned and hastened back to the cafe.

Le Rennet was gone, the table cluttered with crumpled franc notes. But the woman remained. With a greasy hand she grasped my arm, led me to the door and pointed in the opposite direction from which I had come.

As I followed the street's turns, my anxiety increased, especially as I considered the footpads who seemed literally to take over Paris after nightfall. The neighborhood grew disreputable and I was accosted in my pursuit several times. Fortunately, my accosters were merely women of the evening, and I speedily extricated myself from their solicitations. Finally I espied him, a dim but recognizable figure on a rare straight stretch of the street. Running, I overtook him. He affected not to notice my presence and we walked in silence; he purposefully, I somewhat dazed and out of breath. I believe an hour must have passed before we stopped—at the side entrance to a graveyard.

Noisily, Le Rennet shook the iron gate. A watchman appeared and opened it. A few coins changed hands. I found myself possessed of a lantern. I needed it, but the old man did not. He was at home here, moving steadily between tombs, vaults, and simple markers until he reached his goal. I leaned against the stone and the lantern's rays fell on the name: CHARLES BAUDELAIRE.

"Anywhere, out of this world!" Le Rennett's voice was almost sepulchral. "Charles wrote that. He understood perfectly. Was there anything, I wonder, that he did not understand and make poetry of?"

"A friend?"

"Charles, a friend? No, Master Griswold, a brother. It is one of the greatest sorrows of my life that I never met him."

I had no time to inquire into his strange family connections, for he continued, addressing the monument, or so it seemed. "I was drunk, drugged, ill from exposure, and possessed of some dozen stabbings in my body when I was brought into that hospital. More dead than alive, I was. I had to admit defeat. I had to admit that they had won. The thought nearly put the marker on my grave. My life had been wasted, Griswold, wasted. I even thought of suicide. Not that I had any positive disgust toward life itself, but that I was finally harassed beyond endurance by the adventitious miseries attending upon *my* life. It was while I lay in the hospital, wishing to live yet wearied with life, that I determined upon a course of action which seemed my only salvation.

"I decided to die, Griswold. Yet to live—to leave the world, yet continue to exist. Only the cooperation of Dr. Moran was necessary and that was surprisingly easy to achieve. Young Moran had a submerged literary streak, was a member of the Know-Nothing Party, and was as disgusted as I with the decayed body politic of Baltimore. So together we cooked up the story of my death. I had few friends and fewer relatives in Baltimore, just a cousin. They were told that I had a fever, that I was raving incoherently, and finally that I was dead. But I was heavily bandaged and spirited to the bed of a man about my general stature. An itinerant tinker he was, named Hans Pfaall, who failed to survive the ministrations of a Baltimore election crew. His body was moved to my bed, then into my coffin, and then quickly into my grave. On October 9, 1849, Edgar Allan Poe was buried and forgotten."

"But this is plainly impossible," I protested. "All the world knows—" Le Rennet suddenly straightened up, cleared his throat and declaimed to an unhearing audience of graves: "Yes, my friends. A besotted genius within whom the Muse and the god of wine constantly fought, until his body was left a ravaged battlefield! Take warning, all, from his tragic example!" His words sent a shiver through me, for they were quite familiar, the very words, in fact, with which Dr. Moran had concluded his lecture upon the death of Poe.

He continued dreamily, "For two weeks I convalesced in safety, pretending delirium in the presence of anyone but Moran. We spoke only in the dead of night, and upon one thing we agreed. Edgar Allan Poe must remain dead to the world. I could not dare even to let Muddy know I was alive, because I knew that damned vulture, your uncle Rufus, would be hovering. For his help, I wrote Moran a lecture describing my own death, the one you so admired and which brought him fame and much fortune. As a sop to his wife I even included my conversion and final peaceful trip into the arms of the Creator. My fellow Americans lapped that up."

A fit of coughing stalled his words, and I grew fearful for his health. "I'm all right," he snarled. "All right. I am still alive." He stumbled, however, and grasped the monument for support. Still, he refused to leave and continued his fantastic tale. "My moustache and hair had been chopped off already. When I determined it would be safe to leave, Moran painted me with some vile-smelling concoction, a purple salve which nearly covered my face. God, I must have looked horrible; people veritably fled my presence. I boarded a packet from Baltimore, and feigned ignorance of any language addressed to me. Once under way, I felt happy, Griswold. For the first time in years, I felt free. Death is indeed the ultimate freedom. Charles knew that."

Throughout his recital I had experienced a severe disorientation: midnight, a graveyard, a *fantast* as Evans had labelled him, and my own inconceivable involvement with him. I seized the moment to interject an element of the practical into this *bizarre* scene. "But after you regained your health, why did you never make your presence known?" I asked.

"They would have killed me!" he shouted. I caught the lantern just before it hit the ground. "Yes, that was true. At least for a while." Le Rennet's voice was subdued now. "Despite some justifiable fear, I nearly declared myself during the late war between the states. Yet . . . You did not understand. Hans Pfaall *enjoyed* his freedom. And then, sadly, I realized I am not what I was. For that I am sorry, Charles." He saluted the monument and shuffled toward the gate.

The following morning I prodded him to continue his fanciful account, demanding to know why anyone would wish to harm the late poet, who, to my knowledge, was his own worst enemy. However, it was now his humor to decline all conversation upon the subject. Several days passed before he was to resume his fantastic tale.

During those days, my sole duty, trotting and fetching for the old man, palled upon my senses. I longed for the adventures of commerce. And to see more of Mery Laurent. Happily she visited at a time when old Le Rennet was out upon some errand which he would not entrust to his *brosseur.* It was early afternoon, and there was a touch of spring in the air. I confessed that I was actually growing fond of Paris. And of her, the gayest of the gay, the most lovely in a city where all were beautiful. I strove to make her comprehend the ardent desire I possessed—so ardent, in truth, that we neither heard the return of Le Rennet. He made no direct comment on our embarrassing condition.

"The second post has arrived. Get your stick, Master Griswold. And straighten your collar." That cursed stick! It was one of Le Rennet's most *outre* beliefs that his investigations were being spied upon. Despite the talk of Taaffe's men, my own vigilance had discovered no suspicious persons lurking about. Yet, to deceive these unseen opponents, he insisted that all communications between the dentist and himself be in cipher. The stick was the key to it.

At first glance one might think it nothing more than a standard sliding rule. Upon closer examination, however, one discovered not Gunter's tables, but the jumbled letters of the alphabet in four rows. Hence, by moving the tongue or slide along the letters of one alphabetic row, the actual meaning of the ciphered message could be read from the letters of a second alphabet in a different row.

The letter from Evans was a lengthy one, running to some four pages. I dreaded dealing with it. The habit of Le Rennet and Evans of intermingling English, French, and German words—plus an occasional word or phrase in Latin or Greek —made such tasks tedious in the extreme. As did the fact that vowels were but rarely used, and had to be deduced from context. When I objected to such ridiculous measures, Le Rennet would invariably counter: "Privacy, Griswold, is not ridiculous. To know the thoughts and questions of your opponent—and to deny him such knowledge of your own mind—such is the essence of success in any project."

The very first line of Evans' message greatly excited Le Rennet—out of all proportion, I then thought, to its content. The message deciphered read:

K S M H T D S P N X

The letter *X* was used to indicate an end to that particular segment of the message. Owing to the old man's insistence that all communication must be written backwards, the letters then had to be reversed:

N P S D T H M S K

I had by this time become sufficiently familiar with the workings of the cipher to successfully complete the message in a few moments by adding the necessary vowels:

NE PAS DEATH MASK

"So. Against all tradition, Rudolph was buried without a death mask being made! Why? Why?"

"Perhaps, sir, it was an oversight. Or the result of undue haste which the tragic event occasioned."

"Perhaps," he said and fell into one of his reveries, leaving me the chore of deciphering the remainder of the message. Further disgruntled by Mery's sudden departure, I accused him of daydreaming away his time. He answered without opening his eyes. "Those who dream by day, Master Griswold, are cognizant of many things which escape those who dream by night. Pray continue your task."

I plodded along and by early evening had completely deciphered the letter. Two more points in particular caused Le Rennet to stir from his lethargy. The first was Evans' discovery that the prescription book of the Court Pharmacy contained a forged page. The forgery was created upon a thinner paper and pasted in the book in place of a missing page. The forged page covered prescriptions issued for the royal family over the past year. I offered no comment upon this, except to point out that if the dentist's observations were accurate, then there surely must be a logical explanation for the inserted page.

"Of course there is, you dunce," spat out Le Rennet. "What do you think we are doing but searching for that explanation?" Having grown accustomed to his outbursts, I made no complaints, and continued my report of Evans' letter.

"According to Evans, Baroness Mary Vetsera died with

Prince Rudolph, an apparent suicide. However, the Emperor claimed that Mayerling was part of the imperial household and therefore not subject to civil laws. On the night of January 31st, her uncle Alexander Baltazzi and another relative dressed the poor girl's body in a fur coat and hat; they transported it sitting between them, in the dead of night, to a cemetery, where she was buried the next morning. No death certificate was issued."

"And what do you think now?" he demanded.

"Preposterous!" I exploded, being nettled by his smugness. "Mere twaddle. Stuff and nonsense! Do you expect me to believe that a sovereign government would condone such a grievous piece of misconduct? Even in Europe? The thought is monstrous."

At this, the old fool again revealed his common origins. He laughed, 'til he choked and spat the wine he was drinking down his shirt front. I attempted reason. "Sir, progress has blessed not only the mechanical arts, but the art of governance as well. In an earlier age, I grant, our politics were somewhat primitive. But this is the dawn of a new era—an era in which the halls of government will be forever free of chicanery and scandal." My efforts were in vain. My hearer alternated between laughing and choking until I feared a recurrence of his seizures.

He controlled himself finally and began to speak in a surprisingly serious tone. Thus was I given a second glimpse into the chimerical history of Henri Le Rennet, the man who claimed to be Poe.

"It was precisely because of your damnable politicians that I was forced to stage my own death. Not that I had any love of the mob, Master Griswold. But those Whigs, as they called themselves, were beyond endurance. They were the newly monied, and advocated a return to the old ways. The secret caucus rather than the open convention. Backroom boys, all of them. They sought to reimpose qualifications to vote, to hold office, and the like. Not qualifications based upon proven merit, but upon their own positions—so they might pass laws to protect their own treasure boxes.

"But I had them beaten. For years I had painfully pursued one goal, the publication of a magazine. *The Stylus,* it was to be called. It would appeal to the intelligence of all men and become not simply a literary beacon, but a mighty political force as well. 1849, Griswold. Viriginia was dead. Muddy and I were still in New York, living in that hovel in Fordham. We had sold everything—furniture, clothes, the lot. We existed mostly on dandelions Muddy gathered and made into a soup, 'It's good for you, Eddie. It cools the blood.' God what she suffered. But by the end of that wretched summer I had collected nearly one thousand subscriptions from men of insight and vision who had guaranteed the success of my magazine by promising a full year's payment in advance as soon as the first issue was printed. The names were copied carefully by Muddy and me on a master list. That list was guarded like the treasure it was. I carried it with me everywhere in an old satchel. In August of 1849, an offer of solid financial backing for the first issue arrived. I knew that I had won."

He paused for breath and more wine. I joined him in a glass, and he proposed an odd toast. "To *The Stylus.* Nevermore." He fell into a moody silence. "But what happened, sir?" I asked quietly, for will I nill I, his story fascinated me.

"I decided upon one more trip—to Richmond, where I was well known. A few lectures, and more subscriptions. But I grew intemperate. I bruited my success about, in the wrong quarters. And Rufus Griswold, your damnable uncle, he heard."

"Are you determined to slander the dead, sir?" I protested vigorously.

"Your uncle was a small man, Master Griswold. He despised the ideals of Jefferson, of Jackson. He was a true Whig from his bald pate to his spats. He could gain stature only by keeping better men beneath his boot." Brushing aside my further objections, he continued his narrative. "I took the old noonday side-wheeler from New York to South Amboy. I planned to go from there by train to Baltimore, and then to Richmond by steamer. It was the cheapest route at the time, and I was as poor as a rat. It began on the train. I shall never forget the cheek of those two scoundrels. They seated themselves behind me and talked openly about their plans to kill me."

"You must have mis-heard," I suggested reasonably.

"I did not mis-hear, and those two were not speaking in jest!"

"What did you do?"

"I did what any sane man would do under the circumstances. I pretended I was mad. I made such a commotion that their plans were foiled and they left the train at Bordentown. I continued to feign madness, thus gaining time to think. Those two villains were quite specific: they wanted my list of subscribers and would kill me to get it. In Philadelphia, I had to change to the Baltimore train. I had but little baggage, my satchel and an old trunk with my meager clothes. I placed my precious satchel in the hands of a porter with instructions that it be kept until I called for it personally. I carried my trunk with me. My fears were justified. A friend—a supposed friend—insisted upon hearing my tale over a bottle of wine. Inside the railroad saloon, the man seated next to us claimed that I had stolen fifty dollars from his pocket. I spent the night in jail. When I was released the next morning my trunk was returned to me—the lock broken. As soon as I could safely do so, I retrieved my satchel and took the train to Baltimore."

"Aha!" I exclaimed mockingly. "And I presume your every movement was observed, that sinister fellows followed you everywhere."

"There was no need. My destination was no secret. When

I arrived in Richmond, I knew they were there. I tell you I could feel them, but damn me if I knew who they were. I secured thirty-two additional subscribers in Richmond, and determined to set off at once. A group of admirers invited me to spend my final night at a supper to celebrate the great success of a lecture on poetry I had given the previous evening. I was able to leave their company briefly. I returned to my hotel and substituted bits of my clothing for the subscription list in the satchel. The list was placed in the trunk, beneath some old volumes. Deliberately, I left the trunk lid open, and hid the satchel beneath my bed.

"We drank away the evening and the early morning too. It was barely dawn when, dragging my trunk, I teetered down the dock, boarded the steamer, and was cheered on my way. A friend was supposed to have placed my satchel on board. Naturally when I inquired it was nowhere to be found. The worst was over, I thought. And I still had my subscriptions. But I had forgotten that when we ported at Baltimore, it would be election time.

"He introduced himself as Henry Reynolds, and claimed to have a message from your uncle. In my confusion, I suspected nothing. He offered to provide clothing, which I sorely needed. He was informed of my project, he said, and wished to help. It was an easy matter. A heavily drugged glass of wine. And another. And another. I awoke in a coop of repeaters. The windows were boarded and two villains with drawn pistols stood at the door. They were the same two who had been on the train. I was overcome first with the suffocating smell of human filth, then with a thirst for laudanum and brandy which caused me to shake uncontrollably until the need was supplied. For most of the next day, we travelled from one Whig election poll to another. Some thirty or more barely recognizable human beings, we would walk to the voting window, mumble a name—any name at all—and repeat the only words which would get us more brandy. 'A Whig. Mark me a Whig.' When we came to the last stop on our rounds—the Fourth Ward I learned later—there was Reynolds. A Whig election judge. He called to the coop warden. I was pulled aside and made to understand that I would be last in the line. As I staggered toward the poll, a mob closed in upon me. I felt excruciating pain, from every side, as I was stabbed again and again. I fainted. And awoke to the face of Dr. Moran."

So involved had I become in the intricacies of his narration that I waited for some minutes before I realized that he intended to speak no more.

"But what had my uncle Rufus to do with your adventures? I fail to see how he was in any way concerned, despite what your Mr. Reynolds might have said."

"When I planned that last trip, I was buoyant with the knowledge that *The Stylus* would exist. No. I was aloft, soaring, my treasure visible in the jewelled skies. I did not think. Even if I had—but I did not—I would have found your uncle's slight generosity an attempt to ingratiate himself, his eyes to the future. No connection, Master Griswold? It was your uncle, Rufus Wilmot Griswold, who purchased my tickets. He alone knew my itinerary." Le Rennet arose, drained his glass, and retired.

"Why would a few names on a subscription list be of interest to a powerful political party?" I asked on the following morning. "Agreed, history is filled with examples of a handful of men changing the course of events. That glorious scene at Thermopylae, for example—"

"It wasn't just the subscribers, Griswold. It was the fact that I, Edgar Allan Poe, would be editor of *The Stylus* and its major contributor!" He grasped my hand with a nervous *empressement*. "That is what the Whigs could not tolerate."

Not satisfied, I requested further details, but Le Rennet had other plans for the day, and it was at least another week before the final veil was drawn to disclose the conclusion of his fanciful story.

The occasion was the old fellow's sudden desire for a gumbo. Despite his small stature, his fraility, and his obvious years, Le Rennet displayed at table a gusto which was prodigious. He frequently had me toiling over an ancient iron stove which occupied a corner in his makeshift kitchen. His special delight was a gumbo which he claimed to have originated and which, according to his own modest judgment, was superior to the creations of the finest *chefs* in Paris.

"We must purchase a chicken, Griswold." So it began, and we were off that morning traipsing through the streets in search of a fresh chicken. Any hint of spring warmth had vanished. March winds whipped violently about us. Oblivious to them, Le Rennet stopped at every bookstall along our route and casually thumbed through the castoff volumes, while I shivered and cursed the inventor of the printing press. At one such stall, he let out a whoop, and waving a slight volume, gave the seller what was asked without argument— rare indeed, for Le Rennet took special delight in that French custom of haggling over prices.

"There is your answer, Griswold!" He handed me the volume. However, since I was carrying a chicken and a basket of oysters, I could but imperfectly grasp it. He held it before my eyes. It was a French edition of some stories by Edgar Allan Poe. "I'll autograph it for you sometime. Probably out of print in my own country, damn them!" He opened the volume to its contents page and pointed. I could make little of the line his quivering finger touched. It was a story apparently about a man who was destroyed or some such thing.

"Used up. *The Man that Was Used Up!* I wrote it." Nervously I shifted the chicken and noted with distaste that some blood had seeped through the paper and was dribbling down my trousers. He straightened his shoulders, turned about smartly, and marched off. As I followed, he began to *sing*! His voice cracked a bit, but he made up in enthusiasm and volume what he lacked in musical delicacy. He was so tickled that he repeated the verse over and over again, until it was impressed upon my memory:

> Sir Walter is a noble Scott
> Who writes of life on the heathers.
> General Winfield is a dreary Scott,
> Known not for tales but feathers.

We formed such an odd procession that it was with great relief I entered our lodgings.

Le Rennet pulled the cork from a bottle of wine, and I started to prepare his gumbo. The old fellow was in a cheerful mood. "I met him at the Point," he said. "It was late fall."

"Whom did you meet?" I asked, while pitching more charcoal into the stove. Soon the chicken, chopped into pieces, was at a full boil.

"Why, General Winfield Scott. He was a fine figure of a man, stood six and one-half feet at least. He was reviewing the troops, all creased, barbered, with his leather gleaming. The very perfection of a military man. Old Fuss and Feathers, they called him. And a stickler for military punctilio. Why if he found a trooper drunk, do you know what he would do?"

I admitted my ignorance as I stirred the chicken and spooned off the scum. "He would have the poor soul dig his own grave and stand in it from sun-up to sun-down, with the firm understanding that if he were ever found drunk again, General Scott would personally see to it that he would occupy the grave—permanently."

"Were you detected drunk?" I asked, still stirring.

"Worse. Naturally, the crowd at Benny Havens' could not tolerate him. And on the night of the review, I stood upon a table and sang my latest composition. I was well known even then for my poetic talents, having often amused my fellow cadets with my rhymes about our officers." Here the old man did actually climb upon the table, nearly landing his foot in the basket of oysters, and repeated the verse he had been singing. "But there were no cheers when I finished. I discovered cadets bolting toward doors, windows, the cellar. And before me stood Old Fuss and Feathers himself!"

I rescued the oysters. " 'You are a disgrace, sir!' boomed General Scott, and he struck me, reaching my face even though I was standing upon that table. It was not a hard blow, just a slap. But I was put on report and my life made miserable. Soon after, I left West Point for good." I assisted him down from his perch and he sat quietly for a moment, studying his glass of wine. "Well, Griswold, that was when I began writing for a livelihood—if you could call my constant wretched condition living. And I followed General Scott's career with personal interest. As my fortunes declined, his rose. He was breveted a general and became a public hero. The Man of the Hour, he was called everywhere, and his name was spoken with a religious fervor which you would scarcely credit to a democratic people. So I wrote that story. It was published in the *Messenger* and caused quite a stir." Here he chuckled and fell into a fit of coughing so that it was several moments before he could resume. I opened the oysters, gashing my hand on the last one. "The Man of the Hour," I prompted, before he could comment on my inepititude.

"Yes, *The Man that Was Used Up*. In that story I described a general, a public hero, just like Scott. But my general was just 'an exceedingly odd-looking bundle of something' which lay upon his bedroom floor. Only with the help of his servant, who inserted false teeth, false eyes, false hair, everything false, only then was the great man recognizable in his public image. He was indeed a hollow man, a man used up."

I bandaged my hand as best I could and plopped the oysters with their juice into the pot. I remarked casually that I seemed to recall a General Scott who had made some name for himself in the histories for his campaigns against the Indians and rebellious Mexicans. But I declared I could see little in that *bizarre* story to endanger its author. "It might be considered in poor taste, sir, but hardly a threat to a national figure."

"But that was just the beginning, Griswold. At my own expense. I reprinted that story a few years later, in the first volume of my projected collection of all my fictions. But my finances permitted only the initial volume to be published. I was delighted, nonetheless, that Scott's story was in print again. I kept at it. I followed his career closely, revising the tale, adding, changing, bringing it up to date. There was more bite with each revision and the final version, completed in 1849, was a masterpiece, even if I do say so myself. It presented General Winfield Scott as the hollow, insipid, thoughtless, witless fool he truly was. And this was the tale which I planned to include in the very first number of *The Stylus*. It would have been sensational. Because of it, I was marked for death by the Whigs."

My confusion only deepened. I fear I lost count of the number of spoons of powdered sassafras leaves. "I still fail to understand," I said, just as Le Rennet roughly jerked the spoon from my hand. "Because, you dunce, precisely twenty-three spoons full will season and thicken the dish to perfection. Any more will ruin it."

"I meant about General Scott," I protested, stirring madly to mix the broth and leaves. Then I pushed the pot to the back of the stove and put on the rice.

"Yes, you would have a short memory," he mumbled. "In 1849, in the backest of backrooms, it had already been arranged that General Winfield Scott, the Man of the Hour, was to be the Whig Party's candidate for the President of the United States. He was nominated at Institute Hall, in your noble Baltimore, in 1852. Fortunately our countrymen showed enough good sense to deny him and his party a victory in that election, even though I failed to show them why."

"Then you maintain that General Scott attempted to assassinate you, or rather, Edgar Allan Poe."

"Naturally not. Scott was used up. He was merely an attractive figure around which to rally the Whigs. He knew nothing of the plot. He knew next to nothing of anything. The rice is boiling over." He filled his glass again and set two plates upon the table. The gumbo was delicious.

CHAPTER

4

That motley drama!—oh, be sure
It shall not be forgot.

BUT MAN DOES NOT LIVE BY GUMBO ALONE. I GREW INCREAS-
ingly restless. The days were fleeting—as were my funds. The
Exposition was about to open. "What of Bob's Oil?" I demanded, and my aged companion relented. Together we
would canvass in the hope of drumming up business. In the
morning's sunshine, Eiffel's tower reached heavenward, while
at our feet flowers peeped above the soil. A brisk wind
snapped the flags and banners which dressed the streets. An
aura of galvanic excitement seemed to grip the populace.
Commerce was in the air!

The first hour was not fruitful. Hampered by my missing
teeth and the perversities of the French language, my explanations of the efficacy of Bob's Oil produced naught but laughter. "Follow me," ordered Le Rennet, and he led me, not to
a pharmacy or barbering shop, but to a cafe. "Wait," he said,
pointing toward a vacant table. He removed a bottle from a
sample case and engaged the proprietor in an animated conversation. He returned, handing me several crumpled bills.
"A deposit. Remainder payable upon delivery. A great gross

of your largest bottles. To be shipped immediately." He walked out. The proprietor nodded and grinned inanely at me.

"Truly an epic feat," I enthused when I caught up with Le Rennet. "How did you accomplish it so quickly?"

"I merely pointed out that there is a heavy tax upon spirits but none upon hair oil. Since your tonic contains more alcohol than most brandy, plus some harmless herbs which produce a flavor not unlike British gin . . . well, he saw my point at once."

I protested vehemently that such a use of my father's life's work was intolerable. "But think of it, Griswold: Bob's Oil will be the greatest success of the Exposition," he assured me.

"Well, perhaps there are precedents," I said. Further discussion was cut short, for there were two missives awaiting us when we reached our abode. The first was from Evans, and required fiddling with the cipher stick. Fortunately, it was brief:

AUTOPSY CONFIRMS SUICIDE

"The fools," muttered Le Rennet, and reached for wine.

The second message was more to his satisfaction. In an envelope pushed beneath our door was an engraved calling card: Frederick, Baron von Metzengerstein. He was, the card announced, chief of protocol at the Embassy of Austria, Paris. On the reverse, written in English, I read: "Tonight at 19:00 hours." Below was scribbled an address in a remote quarter of the city.

"A real baron, or a hoax?" I asked.

"The question is, whose baron or whose hoax." To my amazement he actually set about performing an elaborate toilet, brushing his wild hair into some semblance of order about his crown, changing into fresh linen. "I must purchase some clothes," he announced. "When entertained by a baron one must be suitably prepared."

Our destination was a short distance away, a dilapidated

store which sold castoff apparel. After much consultation with the clerk, Le Rennet chose a three-button cutaway frock coat with a notched collar. It was of black cassimere with faint blue threads. The few alterations necessary were speedily completed. I must admit that in his new coat and complementary pants, the old fellow cut a surprisingly elegant figure.

"Why one would scarcely recognize you, sir!" I offered most sincerely. "How truly is it said that clothes make the man."

"*Sometimes*, Master Griswold," he replied tersely.

No further communications awaited us upon return, and, since it was early afternoon, I declared for a brief nap to refresh myself for this evening's entertainments. I was awakened some hours later by a clatter at our door. "Well!" I shouted rudely as I jerked the portal open. There stood Mery. Though I was collarless and dishevelled, she appeared not to notice. "Where is Henri?" she asked, brushing past me. "Hello, hello," I said, still drowsy, but greatly pleased. However, thoughts of dalliance were soon dispelled. "Henri is not here? But you promised. And I have news of importance." Her pout was so enchanting that I had great difficulty concentrating upon what she related.

Her news was this. By way of a friend who was a director of the *Compagnie Internationale des Wagons-Lit*, Mery had learned that a Vicomte de Montreine had reserved passage from Brindisi, by train, for the evening of February first. She was visibly excited, though I could see little of interest.

"This, then, was the same Vicomte de Montreine who had told the priest a fanciful story of Rudolph's suicide?"

"But of course. It must be, *n'est-ce pas?*"

"And where did he travel to?"

"Aha! Supposedly to Brussels. Yet the porter swears he was never on the train."

"But what does that mean?"

"Tell Henri. He will know. But first you must find him."

With a stern admonition, she planted the briefest of kisses

upon my cheek and left. The bells of St. Germain tolled the hour of five. Hurriedly I dressed and set off in search of Le Rennet—again. I located him eventually in a dingy cafe which we had frequented on several occasions prior. He was in the midst of some boisterous companions whom he seemed to be amusing with some very diverting tale. I caught his eye and waited politely near the door for him to join me. But he continued in the conviviality of that disreputable crowd. I refused the offer of a waiter to be seated, preferring to stand as a reminder of our evening's obligations. At last! Le Rennet left the table and walked past me without a word, silently joining the evening bustle of Parisian streets. As we waited at a corner for a stream of carriages to pass, he broke into my thoughts.

"You are correct, Master Griswold. Such a sloppy waiter should be dismissed at once. But then who would provide for his family?"

I replied that while I was not indifferent to the sufferings of my fellow mortals, such sloppiness bordering upon filth seemed more proper to the workhouse than a thriving public enterprise. I stopped. "How did you know I was thinking of that waiter?"

He only grinned and resumed walking. At my insistence he offered this explanation. "You arrive at the cafe, plainly concerned with the hour. Twice you withdraw your watch, each time comparing it with the large clock mounted below the staircase. But then you stop fidgeting. Your frown becomes one not of annoyance, but introspection. You follow me from the cafe, and you do not chide or chatter but continue lost in your thoughts. What occurred to change your cast of mind? There is only one explanation: the waiter approached and spoke to you. You glared after him. You shot your cuffs, brushed an imagined spot from your coat, straightened your four-in-hand, and fell into your brown study. Marcel's apron is stained, but so are most waiters' aprons in Paris. However, his trousers are unbrushed and unpressed. His shirt, which has not been washed for several days, contains the remnants of meals and wine. Then we pause for traffic and your countenance brightens. Why? A man passed us, the one in the Prince Albert and silk hat. Possibly a banker. Your eye follows him, alighting on a *gendarme* in mid-street, with his spotless uniform and polished boots.

"At this point I interrupted your thoughts. From one narrow point of view, Marcel's appearance is deplorable. But before you judge too harshly, remember that Marcel's wife is a consumptive, dying, Master Griswold, and she cannot wash and iron his linen because of coughing blood. He has four children."

Was he a wizard, or did he simply make a fortunate guess? As we rattled toward our appointment, I pondered this question, and made this judgment: however he arrived at his conclusion, Le Rennet did indeed divine my innermost thoughts. I quitted this frustrating line of speculation and sought to engage my companion in conversation.

"Can we be certain the person we are to meet is actually a baron? That he does represent the Austrian government?"

"If he is a huge hog of a man, with an arrogant bearing, a snub nose and tufts of black hair sprouting from his ears and nostrils, yes, we can be assured he is the Baron Metzengerstein. I spoke with Etienne. The Baron is attached to the Embassy, but works for Taaffe, of course. A subtle man. We must be cautious, Griswold."

My earlier excitement had deserted me, and I was no longer so enthusiastic about meeting a real baron. The cab turned into what appeared to be a private park, covering many acres and heavily wooded. The lane curved before a palacelike affair, with stately columns and immense double doors. We were admitted by a servant whose muscles fairly bulged the buttons and seams of his uniform. Silently, he led us down a corridor lined with works of art, all selected for their portrayal of women. Many, I blush to report, were actually lewd or obscene. My companion was merely amused.

We were ushered into an immense oblong room, carpeted

in rich, liquid material of Chili gold. The furnishings were opulent and continued the same theme of femininity. A gigantic, sparkling crystal chandelier burnished the room. At the far end, behind a massive desk of vermilion and gold, sat the baron.

He approached us with a waddling gait. He was a fat man, beyond all doubt, but with no trace of the jollity one associates with corpulence. He was fifty, perhaps more, and by no means handsome—the reverse, in fact. His face was all harshness, his eyes large, glassy, heavily lidded. His lips gently protruded from his puffy cheeks. Although his pate gleamed, tufts of hair, as predicted, nearly filled his nostrils and ears. His whole air bespoke a petty Caligula, accustomed to shameful debaucheries, flagrant treacheries.

Odd to say, his voice was startlingly soft. "You will inform the Baroness that our guests have arrived," he said, dismissing the servant. "Monsieur Le Rennet," he bowed, and turning to me, "Mister Greasewold."

"Griswold, sir. Wilmot Rufus Griswold. From Maryland."

"I am honored." He bowed deeply, drawing his lips into a hint of a smile. "A brandy, gentlemen?" Without awaiting an answer, he poured three portions. "To a successful evening!" he raised his glass and his voice. "So, I have invited you to my little retreat, as I believe our affairs might better be conducted away from the embassy. Informally, yes? I have been ordered upon All-Highest Command—" here, he stiffened and snapped his heels "—to assist you, Monsieur Le Rennet. But . . . I am frankly puzzled. Concerned, yes, concerned." He swirled the brandy in his glass.

He continued, picking his words with exaggerated care. "Our Most Gracious Majesty is well known for her . . . eccentricities. But this? To claim there is some . . . mystery about the deeply lamented death of the Crown Prince? And to cause so many people such . . . labors?" He paused, awaiting a comment.

"An excellent brandy, Baron," said Le Rennet, holding his goblet to the light.

"The first pressings of forty-eight were superb. I doubt if we shall see their like again." He smiled. "*Touche*. Much we know, of course. After all, it would be . . . unrealistic . . . to suppose the movements of an Empress could be concealed indefinitely. And much we can guess. Really, Monsieur Le Rennet! At this moment in history . . . a dentist? How suddenly the royal teeth need care. And those humorous messages. They present a welcome challenge to the cipher officers at the Foreign Ministry. But it shall only be a matter of time. Shall we . . . cooperate? In matters of state, is not the choice: cooperation or war?"

"I had hoped we could cooperate, Baron." Le Rennet drained his glass, and it was immediately refilled. "You have received certain papers . . . letters, journals, written by the Crown Prince."

"Yes, yes, and I am to allow you to read these most private documents. But I am compelled by my duty to dissuade you from such a course." He sighed hugely. "Monsieur, you must be aware of how an unbridled press may whip up wild fancies. How in pandering to popular prejudices, these fanciful notions are caused to grow among the ignorant. Resulting, always, in vulgar errors."

"But, Baron, I am no journalist. Surely you know that."

"Yes, we have made inquiries. Discreetly."

"Naturally."

"You do have a certain reputation, Monsieur Le Rennet. Two reputations, in fact. In some quarters, you are considered . . . a genius . . . of sorts. Your assistance to the Paris Prefecture is acknowledged. Privately, of course. Yet others maintain a different opinion. My duty as a host forbids I repeat their views. You discern my dilemma. How would the Hapsburg Empire benefit were I to turn over to your scrutiny the most personal papers of our beloved late Crown Prince?"

"Discipline, Baron. Discipline. Is not their Serene Majesties' domain held together by discipline? By unquestioning obedience to orders?"

"Are you determined to be difficult, Monsieur Le Rennet?" Before an answer was forthcoming, however, the door opened. The Baron's countenance brightened. "Ida, my dear. Won't you join us? Gentlemen, may I present my wife, Ida Illyes, Baroness von Metzengerstein."

What am I to say? If Mery Laurent was lineally descended from Eve, from whom did the Baroness descend? Adam? Impossible. But then whom? She was willowy, with jet-black short curls and raven lashes of great length. Her skin was powdered a ghostly white, with a touch of carmine on her cheeks. But she was dressed in ministerial black, in a smartly tailored man's suit. A man's shirt and collar was set off with a black cravat. A gold watch chain shone across her waistcoat.

"Charmed, Madame Baroness, I have never seen—" She turned and spoke harshly. "Why do you whistle when you speak?" I flushed. "But do not be embarrassed. It amuses me, and you must always amuse me." She produced a cigar from a case, and the Baron moved with surprising swiftness to set it aflame, with some curious mechanical device.

Her mannerisms were jerky, puppetlike. She turned to Le Rennet. "So. You are the one who would know of Rudolph?"

Le Rennet acknowledged her question with a slight bow. "Did you know the Crown Prince, Baroness?"

"Of course I knew him! I am Hungarian." I could not follow the logic of her statement, but I noted upon closer examination certain indisguisable Slavic features. "Permit me to explain," interjected the Baron. "My wife is of a very ancient and once powerful Hungarian family. Before she consented to become the Baroness von Metzengerstein, she moved in youthful circles where there was much talk of Hungarian independence. I believe the late Crown Prince also, at times, moved in the same circles. But that is all in the past, is that not so, Ida?"

"Certainly," she answered sharply.

"How shall we entertain our guests, my dear?" To answer his own question, the Baron removed two packs of playing cards from their case. "Do you play, Monsieur Le Rennet?" he asked with studied casualness.

"Vint?" asked my old companion equally casual.

"Yes, one may win a great deal of money at Vint. Or lose."

"From personal experience, Baron, I can attest to both facts."

As if to illustrate his point, the Baron returned to that massive desk, unlocked a drawer, and removed a thick packet of bills. "My wife and I shall be partners, of course. Shall we say ten francs a point?" I protested my ignorance of the game, as well as my limited supply of funds. "It is a simple variant of bid whist, Griswold," explained Le Rennet. "And I shall stand your losses."

"Excellent!" exclaimed the Baron. Chairs were brought; the packs shuffled. More brandy was poured. The Baron again fingered his stack of bills. "Yes, one can make a great deal of money at Vint. It all depends upon what one does. I wonder what you will do, Monsieur Le Rennet?"

"I shall bid one, no trump," answered the old man, fumbling with his cards. We lost the hand. And the game. And continued to lose. Le Rennet seemed hardly conscious of the cards.

"You play clumsily, Monsieur. Distracted? Does something trouble you?" asked the Baron.

"I was thinking of Mary Vetsera," answered my partner, and in that dreamy voice he at times affected, he continued, "A dirge for her, the doubly dead, in that she died so young."

"She was a silly, romantic fool," exclaimed the Baroness, slapping a trump eagerly upon the trick.

"But still a pity, Ida, my dear. She had yet to celebrate her eighteenth birthday. . . . And to so tragically end her own life."

"There is no doubt it was suicide?" asked Le Rennet.

"Absolutely none," said the Baron, a touch of menace in his voice. "I believe that trick is game." He speedily figured upon a pad. "We are ahead by six thousand points, Monsieur," he announced. The old man riffled the pile of notes before him, and said, "I believe we have sufficient for another game or two. Perhaps our luck will undergo a change, Master Griswold."

"Perhaps you would care to increase the stakes?" suggested the Baron.

"Nonsense," snapped Ida Illyes. "It would be unfair to our guests."

"Then the decision shall be our guests'," countered the Baron. "The choice is yours, Monsieur."

"Fifty francs per point then. You fully believe the account of Loschek, Baron?"

The Baron scowled at his cards, then at Le Rennet. "Johann Loschek entered service at the Court nearly thirty years ago as an apprentice gamekeeper. Two decades ago he was appointed personal gun bearer and loader to Prince Rudolph. He held that position until 1883, when he was promoted to personal valet and Keeper of the Outer Door. His loyalty to the Crown Prince cannot be questioned."

"Pass," said the Baroness. "It is your bid, Mister Griswold."

"One heart," I said hurriedly, caught up in the Baron's explanation. "But do not cases of jealousy occasionally appear, where the servant feels that the qualities of his master are overrated and his own superior? No man is a hero to his own valet," I added.

"You are an American," smirked Ida Illyes, "and can never understand the subtle relationship between master and servant. Is that not true, Frederick?"

"I must pass," growled the Baron, ignoring her question. "Seven hearts," said Le Rennet, and I gasped. But the old man seemed uninterested in the game and continued to question Loschek's veracity. As the play progressed, he pressed the Baron upon that subject.

"You chase after the wind," insisted the Baron wearily. "Why would Loschek lie? He had nothing to gain. His account is attested to by witnesses of unimpeachable character."

"Prince Philip of Coburg and Count Hoyos?" asked Le Rennet.

"What I now will tell you is . . . highly delicate. Loschek found the Crown Prince's vestibule door locked from the inside. He pounded upon the door repeatedly with his fists, then with a wooden log. There was no answer. He sent word by the warden to Count Hoyos, who hurried to the hunting lodge from his own quarters across the courtyard. Count Hoyos suggested that the door be forced, but Loschek then informed him that the Prince was not alone, that Baroness Vetsera was with him. At this moment, Prince Philip arrived and was fully informed of the situation. Both agreed that Loschek should batter the door open without delay. He did, and found that the door to the Prince's bedroom was also locked. Upon their authority, Loschek smashed the bedroom door. He splintered one panel, looked inside, and nearly fainted from shock. 'They are both dead!' he cried. Loschek was ordered to reach inside the broken panel, open the door, and convince himself that all life had left them. This he did, and returned moments later with the tragic news. Mary Vetsera and Crown Prince Rudolph were dead. You may depend upon it, Monsieur Le Rennet, that is the truth. I, myself, have seen the sworn protocol of Count Hoyos."

"I believe we have made a slam, Baron," said Le Rennet, scooping in the final trick. "Odd, is it not, that if Rudolph were planning to commit suicide he would invite two friends to accompany him on a hunt the very same morning."

Ida Illyes laughed stridently. "Not at all odd if you knew Rudolph. Besides, they were not friends. Oh, they would dress up like little soldiers and parade with Rudolph. They rode with him, they hunted bear with him, they told smutty stories and drank beer with him—"

"I doubt our guests are interested, Ida," said the Baron blandly.

"Count Hoyos and Prince Philip are more at home in a stable than a palace. They knew nothing at all of his thoughts, his ideals. Szeps was a friend. Teleki was a friend. Salvator, he was a friend."

The table shook as the Baron slammed down the pack of cards he was shuffling. "That will close the conversation!" he fairly shouted. "Forgive me, my dear Ida, but I do not want the affairs of the Hapsburgs to become the common gossip of the rabble. Those incidents are past and forgotten." Impatiently, he scribbled upon the score pad. "It would seem your luck has improved, Monsieur. In total, you are over 6,000 points the winner. Is that amount sufficient?" His contempt was obvious as he spoke.

"And the documents, Baron? I too would appreciate the opportunity of understanding the late Crown Prince, his thoughts, his ideas."

"I do not believe that will be possible. Not until I get further authorization."

"In that case, Baron, may I suggest one last hand? For higher stakes."

"So. You do have your price. Name it."

"Not in francs, Baron. But in—what was your word?— cooperation? I will either have free access to Prince Rudolph's personal papers, or I shall abandon my efforts altogether."

The Baron pondered this odd proposition, pouring brandy. "Done!" he declared at last. "But only one hand. Then I shall be rid of your meddling. I have your word, sir?"

"You do," replied Le Rennet, in his courtliest manner. "And I have yours?"

"You need not ask. I believe it is your deal, Mister Griswold."

"Concentrate, Mister Griswold," said Le Rennet, unnecessarily, I thought. I realized the importance of this play, but it was his whimsy which had proposed the gamble. Nonetheless, I did feel obligated to perform my best, and nervously I gathered in each card, arranged them, counted my tricks carefully. I possessed a more than biddable hand but desired to learn my partner's strength, so I opened with a deliberately low bid.

"One spade," I said firmly.

"Two spades," said the Baron, chuckling aloud. "Indeed, you should concentrate or learn to count, Mister Griswold."

"Nothing, a pass," said Le Rennet. Ida Illyes stared at him, curiously. "But you have not even looked at your cards, Monsieur. Are you making a joke?"

Deliberately, Le Rennet removed his hands from the table. His cards remained where I had dealt them, in a jumble before him, face down.

"My apologies, Baroness. I choose to play my opponents, not the cards."

"Three spades," said the Baroness with an edge to her voice.

I had absolutely no idea what the old man was getting at. His enigmatic words simply made me angry. Again, I mentally counted my honors, determined to make the best of this absurd situation on my own. I could make one more bid. "Three clubs," I said, and I fear there was a tinge of disgust in my voice.

"Your partner, at least, seems determined to make a game. And you, Monsieur Le Rennet? Will you continue to ignore your cards? Four hearts," said the Baron, carefully closing the fan of his cards and placing them before him on the table. "It is up to you, Monsieur."

Le Rennet's cards remained untouched before him. "Four no trump," he said. "Your feint has failed, Baron."

Ida Illyes threw her cards upon the table. "I pass," she said.

"Pass," I said.

"Pass." The Baron's voice was all iron. "It is your play, Monsieur."

"I play the ten of diamonds," said Le Rennet, his hands still folded on his knees.

"Do you dare? Do you trifle with me?" the Baron boomed.

"I asure you, Baron, I am quite in earnest. But apparently my mind was wandering. Forgive me. Indulge an old man. I meant the ten of hearts." No one spoke. He repeated, "I play the ten of hearts," and pointed at a vacant spot on the table.

"But how droll," said Ida Illyes, placing an ace of hearts upon the invisible ten. I followed suit with a three, and in exasperation, the Baron placed a five upon the cards and swept them in. "Very well, one trick!" he snarled. Ida Illyes led a low spade, which I topped with a nine. Giggling, the Baron gently dropped a king of spades upon the table. Le Rennet indicated he would play a three. We lost that trick and the next one, which Ida Illyes won with the ace of spades. "Three tricks," said the Baron triumphantly. "You can lose no more."

And fantastic as it may sound, we took every remaining trick, making our bid and winning the game. As each succeeding round was played, old Le Rennet would carefully collect the three cards, verbally adding his own card. He placed each trick in a row before him. "Impossible," said the Baron. He turned over each of Le Rennet's cards, and following the old man's instructions, placed it upon the proper pile. "The sixth trick, Baron, taken with the queen of diamonds from my own hand." Finally all thirteen cards were turned and played as Le Rennet had called without even seeing them. The Baron became more furious. He examined the backs of the cards for markings. "But they are your own cards, Baron."

Ida Illyes fell into a frolic, became nearly insane in her laughter. "He has beaten you, Frederick. He has won." She leapt about the room in a macabre imitation of a dance, singing, "Won, won, the Monsieur has won."

It was difficult to tell whether the Baron was more incensed by his inexplicable loss or the laughter of Ida Illyes. Composing himself with great strain he said, "My carriage shall see you home. I will send word when the Prince's papers may be conveniently viewed. Good night, gentlemen." He turned on his heel and literally marched out of the room.

In the carriage, as we clopped through the deserted, echoing streets, I excitedly bade Le Rennet to explain. "A remarkable performance, sir. It truly staggers the imagination."

"Some imaginations, perhaps. But the truly imaginative person is never otherwise than analytic. And my little parlor game was simply a method of obtaining what I could not, in all probability, obtain by other means. To an analytic mind, it would seem absurdly simple."

"Still, sir, it was, well . . . astounding. I play but little, I admit. Yet I have never seen—"

He cut in upon my remarks, and grew expansive upon the subject. "Whist has long been known for its influence upon what is termed the calculating power; and men of the highest order of intellect have been known to take an apparently unaccountable delight in it, while eschewing chess as frivolous. Beyond doubt, Griswold, there is nothing of a similar nature to whist which so greatly tasks the faculty of analysis, of mind struggling with mind."

"But how could you have guessed what cards your hand held?" I demanded hotly, put off by his answer.

"Guess, Griswold?" he snapped. "I do not guess. I observe. I analyze. I use my powers of ratiocination to their fullest. The information is there for everyone, of course, but only the analyst knows what to observe. The analytic player examines the countenance of his partner, comparing it carefully with that of each of his opponents. I suggested, for example, that you play carefully, and what did you do? You gritted your teeth, lips pulled taut, and counted every honor in your hand twice—as you always do when you have an excellent hand. The analytic player considers how each person customarily sorts his hand. Invariably, you put all cards of a suit together. Then, starting from the right, you arrange the suits in descending order according to their strength. Having observed the Baron's sorting pattern, I knew that his strong heart bid was a ruse. I could—and did—count trump by trump, honor by honor, the cards you each held, simply by observing the glances bestowed by their holders upon each. I had previously noted and recorded every variation of face as the play progressed throughout the evening. The differences in the expression of certainty, of surprise, of triumph, of chagrin, provided a fund of material for the ratiocinative faculty. When the final round was played, Master Griswold, I was still in full possession of the contents of each hand but one, which the Baron's reaction to my bid quickly supplied. The rest of you might have turned outwards the faces of your cards."

"Amazing," I said weakly.

"Nevertheless, whist is but a game. We have deeper problems. And darker."

We completed our journey in silence: he with his problems and I with the uneasy thought that I was being made a fool of. Twice during the day he had exhibited powers of what he called ratiocination which I found stupefying. Yet his explanations were so simple that I could barely credit their truthfulness. Was I being deceived by some unseen trickery of his? I knew not what to think and retired early.

My uneasy sleep was shattered during the small hours of the morning by a ghastly, terrifying cry of anguish. The sound reverberated throughout that gloomy house. In panic I raced to the old man's room, where I found the door slightly ajar but braced from the inside. His room was well illuminated with candles and a lamp. Through the slight gap between the door and frame I could see him lying upon the bed, still fully clothed. To my horror I saw that his face was covered with blood. The room—what I could see of it—appeared to be empty, and with a prickle of alarm I glanced around me, expecting at any moment to be set upon myself from the enveloping shadows. Then it occurred to me that perhaps he had not been attacked and beaten, but had suffered another seizure and hæmorrhaged. He carried nitrate of amyl pearls for such an emergency, but perhaps the seizure was so sudden he could not secure them.

I pounded upon the door, and heaved my shoulder to it again and again. "Le Rennet. Le Rennet!" I screamed frantically, my gaze searching that motionless figure for some sign of life. "Help! Help!" I called out wildly, throwing myself bodily at the door.

"Sufficient, Griswold. Sufficient," came the old man's voice from within. As I watched in astonishment, he arose from the bed, wiping his face, actually chuckling. "Be calmed. It is only tomato pulp." He pushed aside the bureau which had held the door and I rushed into the room, angrily berating him. "Cruel, sir! How was I to know what was the situation? If you were injured—or worse, if you were dead?"

"Precisely," he spoke softly, hissing the syllables. "How could you know? Looking through a partially opened door, at a distance of not less than four yards, how *could* you know if I were alive or dead? How could you *know*?" he repeated, now nearly shouting. "Yet, that is precisely the knowledge the servant Loschek claimed. A panel in the door to Prince Rudolph's bedroom is smashed. Loschek peers in. And according to the sworn testimony of Count Hoyos, what does he say? 'They are both dead!' How could he know? Good night, Master Griswold."

CHAPTER

5

Thou wast all that to me, love,
For which my soul did pine—
A green isle in the sea, love,
A fountain and a shrine.

IF THE OLD MAN'S PERFORMANCE UNNERVED ME, IT SENT
Morpheus into headlong flight. Shortly after dawn, I gave up
trying to sleep and arose in a thorough grouch. Having
changed his clothes, Le Rennet had apparently spent the remainder of the night dozing in a chair. I struck a fire and prepared for my toilet, being none too quiet. As I recrossed the
room, he spoke. "I am sorry to have deceived you, Master
Griswold. I had to have your honest reactions."

"You had them, sir," I responded peevishly and re-entered
my chamber. I emerged to find that he had made one of his
tomato concoctions for me, as well as some strong black coffee
accompanied by warmed rolls. This kindness mollified me,
and I inquired if he had found rest during the night. He
replied he had spent the entire time in thought. "You are
exceedingly energetic," I offered.

"I am not energetic. I am desperate."

"Desperate? You have achieved your goal; you have access

to Rudolph's papers. But how that shall change the situation—"

"The situation is that I am an old man, dying a bit day by day; I have little of anything left. Charles said, 'Dear God, grant me the grace to write a few lines of pure poetry, so that I may prove myself superior to those I despise.' I can no longer write a few lines, even a few. My ratiocinative faculties are all I have left, Griswold. I must use them."

While I quietly performed simple household chores, his spirits improved and he discoursed on last evening's subject: the mental agility developed by playing whist. Then the first post arrived. "Vienna," I called out. It took only a few minutes with the cipher stick to interpret the message which touched upon two points, each preceded by NDF. This was their code for an emphatic NO. *N* for *no* and *DF* for *deux fois*, the French for *two times*. The first point concerned the contents of the Crown Prince's bedroom at Mayerling. Evans said that no weapons had been found in it. Similarly, according to the second part of the message, there was no record of a Montreine family.

"Odd," I said. "Yesterday, Mery brought word that Montreine had booked passage upon a train. Yet, according to the porter, he had not even boarded it. I did mean to tell you, but in the rush of events I forgot," I apologized hastily. Already his face signalled a wrathful tirade. Before I completed my sentence, it began. French tumbled from his mouth. "That is rude, sir. You know I cannot understand."

"Let me put it as politely as possible, Màster Griswold. Once a fool, always a fool. Get your hat." We hurried through the streets, finally entering a library of sorts or perhaps it was part of a national museum. The walls were covered with heraldic emblems, which I perused while Le Rennet, in close consultation with a subaltern, pored over volume after dusty volume. Satisfied, he left, taking me to a nearby cafe. The morning's activity and a brandy once more restored his good humor.

"Not in *Debrett,* Griswold, not in *Gotha,* not in any other work, whether for Austria, France, Belgium, England or the remaining states and principalities of Europe. Nowhere is to be found a Vicomte de Montreine, nor a reference to the Montreine family."

"Perhaps the information was erroneous or the name misspelled."

"Perhaps."

"A completely fictitious name would seem an unusual choice for a hoax."

"Unusual, but demonstrating a certain aplomb and wit. Could you invent a completely fictitious name of a titled family, a name which sounded absolutely correct? A name which had never been recorded?" We wandered the streets, the old man deep in thought, saying nothing. His slow but steady gait showed no sign of flagging until I reminded him it was past time for a noon meal.

When we arrived home, we were greeted by Baroness Metzengerstein, today wearing a gray man's suit. She dumped a parcel in my hands, embraced me, and practically pushed us into the house.

"Naturally, I was followed," she said, closing the door by leaning her back into it. "And I have news for you which you should receive in privacy."

For once, old Le Rennet seemed as perplexed as I. "Welcome, Baroness," he finally managed to say.

"What a mad place you live in. I love it. It suits you." She retrieved the parcel from my grasp, removing a bottle of brandy and handing it to me. "For you, my darling." The rest of her parcel she handed to Le Rennet. "And for you. They arrived two days ago from Her Majesty. Quite secretly. Although she did not say so, I assumed they were for you."

Le Rennet fumbled with the wrappings and part of the contents spilled to the floor—three photographs of Rudolph, I learned when I picked them up. "In all," said the Baroness, "there are twenty-six. Gravures, newspaper portraits, royal sittings which were photographed. Twenty-five of Rudolph, one of the Vetsera child. You must have asked for them."

"I did," the old man answered. "And I am grateful. I was unaware you were, how shall I say . . ."

"A spy. For Her Majesty. No need to be delicate. And I perform errands when necessary."

"While the Baron—" Le Rennet began.

"Yes, while the Baron, in addition to his official duties, performs similar services for Taaffe. So, I am followed. But Frederick knows only what I wish him to know. This morning I told my most trusted servant that I was madly smitten with the whistling American I had met last night. I procured a bottle of rare brandy on a pretext, but let her know that it was actually for you." The Baroness met my eyes and smiled boldly. "I am so glad you do not have a beard. Almost everyone does. Such rosy cheeks are delightfully different." So saying, she pinched my right cheek and tugged my chin.

"As is your dress," I replied, shocked but emboldened by her manner.

"Yes," she laughed. "I am myself. An individual. Independent." She uttered the last word with ferocity, then removed a cigar from a pocket and waved impatiently for me to light it. I hurried to the kitchen for matches. The two were seated when I returned. "I am sure the Baron is satisfied. He thinks he knows," she said, patting my cheek as I lit her cigar, "and will not look too closely."

"Your word, Baroness, was *independent*," said Le Rennet while I retreated from the smoke. "Is that the only reason you take risks?"

"Very good, Monsieur. Taaffe and those who serve him are always present. But to work one's own deceptions, however small, is an expression of independence. Rudolph knew that. More, he was a great man who could have made Victor Hugo's dream of a United States of Europe a reality. He could have broken Taaffe's iron ring. Even Franz Joseph is helpless before Taaffe's machinations. The Emperor proposes,

99

his Premier disposes. Yet Taaffe sincerely believes that the only way to keep the Austro-Hungarian Empire together is to keep Hungary subservient. And I am a Hungarian. To be a partner in the Empire, yes. To be a servant, no. So I help Elisabeth. And you."

"What may I do to help you?"

"I want an end put to that rumor which still persists, the belief that Rudolph was killed to prevent him from fomenting revolution, from accepting the crown of Hungary. At the least, such speculation is fruitless, although once it possessed some truth."

"Tell me," said Le Rennet.

"It was years ago." The Baroness paced the room as she talked, waving her cigar. "Rudolph was depressed. Despite his most ardent wishes, his father gave him nothing of significance to do. His inactivity, his inability to put his ideas into effect, the intrigues of the Hofburg and of Taaffe—all disgusted him. His dissatisfaction was known. Count Teleki, a Hungarian nationalist, was prepared to introduce a bill in the Hungarian parliament declaring Prince Rudolph head of the Hungarian army, thus readying the way for his coronation as King of Hungary. Rudolph's close friend, Archduke Johann Salvator, would be appointed Regent of Austria. Moriz Szeps was informed. He edits the *Tagblatt*, a liberal newspaper in Vienna which frequently proposed independence for Hungary. Rudolph himself contributed anonymous articles which took the same position. Szeps carried Count Teleki's offer to the Prince. Though flattered, Rudolph refused. He wanted to create an empire, not destroy one. Such a rash move would set Austria more firmly than ever against Hungary, would bring down reprisals from Taaffe."

"And you believe that is why he killed himself? Depression?"

"I do not! No more than I believe that he was driven to suicide because of his passion for a lovesick child. Look at her." The Baroness snatched the pictures from Le Rennet's hands and found the one she wanted. She flung it at him. I peered over his shoulder, seeing for the first time the features which presumably had driven a Crown Prince to suicide. She was indeed young. Her complexion was unspoiled, her nose turned pertly upward. There was a bow of a smile on her thin lips. Her gaze was direct, beguiling.

"Rudolph met her at Freudenau race course. Last November, think of it! Less than three months before his death. The Turf Angel, she was called. That old lecher the Prince of Wales introduced them. The panderer Countess Larisch arranged later meetings. But Mary Vetsera was not the first, and it is inconceivable that she should have been chosen last! Who was she?" The Baroness shouted her challenge. The tempo of her words increased as she launched herself into a list of Mary's failings. "Her father, Albin Vetsera, a minor diplomatic functionary, was not raised to a baronetcy until ten years ago. He took Mary to Egypt with him where the little fool had an affair with a British officer. She had to be sent home. And her mother's family, the Baltazzis? They own race horses. Mere stable hands. Could the Crown Prince of Austria consider such a liaison? Could the thought of losing the young idiot drive him to suicide? Impossible!" With that, the Baroness threw herself into her chair, crossing her arms in front of her. "A brandy, M. Griswold."

She repelled yet fascinated me. I was embarrassed by her language and complete lack of decorum but almost applauded her theatrics. At a nod from the old man, I went to the kitchen for three glasses. I opened the bottle, then poured. "I took Frederick's best so that he would be certain I was quite serious." She drained her glass before I could hand one to Le Rennet. "Another. Please," she added. "Yes, delightfully different, and so red." She ran an icy finger across my cheek. "The color suits you," she taunted—or so it seemed to me.

"And Prince Rudolph? What suited him? From the pictures, he seems to have experienced difficulty in making up his mind." I was enormously pleased to hear Le Rennet's voice.

"Ah, that was Rudy. He changed as the whim took him. A sailor's beard, a silly Emperor's beard. Then his hussar moustache. Why, once we met in Prague and were walking down the street in front of the military barracks. Three of his officers passed us, but did not salute! They did not recognize him. I thought it was disgraceful and said they should be punished. Rudolph dismissed it as a mere joke, as nothing. Imagine!"

"I shall," said Le Rennet and fell to studying the pictures which were again in his hands.

Just as the Baroness mercifully grew silent, bells marked the hour of two. "You must hurry," she said. "Four o'clock. It is all arranged."

"What is arranged, Baroness?" asked Le Rennet, looking up from the photographs.

"The lecture. At Mondor. A neurology lecture. The note Her Majesty enclosed with those portraits said that it could be of considerable importance to one who is a student of human nature."

"Whose lecture?" I asked.

"Baron Doctor Richard von Krafft-Ebing. He personally treated Rudolph, it is said."

"Excellent," Le Rennet exclaimed. "We must leave at once."

As we were about to depart, the Baroness again embraced me. "I shall go first. It would be better if the Baron did not know of your appointment. Enjoy the brandy." She whistled at me as I stood in the doorway!

We hailed a passing hack and set off for a destination in the suburbs. A hospital, said Le Rennet. One which was famed for its teaching as well as healing.

"And who might this man be?" I asked.

"He is a genius. A Galileo. A Darwin."

"Krafft-Ebing? I have not heard of him."

"You will, Master Griswold."

It was restful to sit in companionable silence, to breathe the spring air recently refreshed by a light rain, to be lulled by the sounds of our travel. A fortunate respite, for when we entered the building, we found ourselves in a current of boisterous students, jostling, joking, waving notebooks, some even singing. Le Rennet asked directions and we turned down a corridor less populated than the rest. We came into a dimly lit wing where a powerful stench of human putrescence made me gasp. Doors stood open. Students were bent over zinc tables, their thin gleaming knives at work on what had once been human shapes.

From a side corridor came groans punctuated by an occasional cry which echoed along the stone walls and seemed to follow us as we proceeded. A patient passed us, wrapped in a blood-spattered gown. With each step his vacant eyes were distorted by pain. My stomach queased and I longed for the clean air. Le Rennet pulled my arm and led me into a large room with seats banked from top to bottom in a semicircle. It was filled to overflowing, so that we were forced to stand against a cupboard in the rear aisle. Behind a chemist's table at the front of the room stood a man who spoke in halting French, some German, and long passages of Latin. Krafft-Ebing, presumably. Despite my knowledge of Virgil's verses, I found myself at a loss as to what he was saying.

His movements were sparse: a raised index finger pointed toward his audience, a glance toward the ceiling as if to capture an escaped word. Otherwise, he stood still, hands behind his back, and droned. I was bored, but alone, apparently, in that response, for when he bowed his head and began collecting his papers, the entire audience rose and softly began to clap their hands. Le Rennet enthusiastically joined them. I had seldom seen the old fellow so excited. "Did you hear, Griswold? I wrote a poem once which spoke about essentially the same phenomenon: the idealization of femininity in its myriad forms."

"Regrettably I understood little of what he said."

"That beggar he treated in Graz. Fascinating. Month after month the beggar saved his alms, all but starving himself. Finally, he would approach a prostitute and take her to a shop where he would buy her an expensive pair of patent leather shoes. He would order her to put them on and walk the streets, wading through as much mud, filth, and manure as could be found. In a hotel room, he would cast himself at her feet and gain extraordinary pleasure from cleaning her shoes with his tongue and lips. That done, he would pay her and return to his miserable existence until he could again save enough to repeat his fantasy. Always the same, always femininity in one of its forms—the shoe, the hat, whatever. Always the idealization of and subjugation to the feminine ideal. Remarkable."

"Disgusting! Rubbish! Either you are jesting with his words or the man is a greater *fantast* than you are. To allow that such practices might exist, even for a moment to allow such a thought, is an affront to human decency. It is unnatural!"

"But how can anything in nature be called unnatural, Master Griswold?"

"And you expect this doctor"—I could hardly say the word —"to have something to say about a Crown Prince, about the heir to the Hapsburg Empire? Incredible. How dare he?"

"Beggars or kings," said Le Rennet. "Beggars or kings." The students had left. Compelled to defend Rudolph's honor and his family's I followed the old hoaxer down the stairs to the table, where he introduced himself.

"Doctor Richard von Krafft-Ebing? Or do you prefer *Baron*?"

"I am here as a doctor," he replied curtly. Although heavily accented, his English proved to be fluent.

"I am Henri Le Rennet. And this is Mr. Wilmot Griswold. You may speak freely in front of him, Doctor."

"I am not sure I should speak at all."

"That is quite understandable." Le Rennet was not perturbed by the man's antagonistic tone. "May I say that I have read your *Psychopathia Sexualis* with great interest? It is an astounding work, sir. It has become a classic in just a short time. Published in 1886, wasn't it?"

"It was. I am pleased that you, who are not a physician, see the merit of my work."

"I do. I believe you were at the University of Graz then, when your treatise was published. An excellent school, though small, providing few opportunities for further research. But now you have been appointed to the chair of neuropathology at the University of Vienna."

"Yes."

"It would be difficult to imagine a better place to continue your work, Doctor."

"It would. To reach the point. I have received a certain communication. What do you wish to know?"

"When did you treat Crown Prince Rudolph?" Silence. I could hear my watch ticking and I believe I held my breath as I watched the two men study each other. So unlike, of course. The old one, small of stature, frail. The other, not so tall as I but stocky and robust. His short hair was a clear brown; only his beard showed occasional gray strands. Had he reached fifty? Yet, like the old one, his hairline was greatly receded and his skin, though firmer, was pouched in the hollows beneath his eyes. There was the true similarity between them —in the eyes: a translucent depth ringed by steel.

"Some three and one-half years ago," Krafft-Ebing answered.

"And the complaint?" Le Rennet spoke softly.

"He did not come from a neurotically degenerate family, as some have suggested. I can assure you that was not the Crown Prince's problem. But even the best bred man is condemned to look upon a woman as the means of satisfying his instinct, unless strong social restraints are imposed. The restraints upon Prince Rudolph were few. Women threw themselves at his feet, at times literally. They acted as if to be possessed by him were a patriotic duty. And the Prince told me that it really *was* their duty. He spoke only partially in jest. His will weakened. From weakness of will, there can only result descent. Degradation. I fear Rudolph surrendered himself to a sensuous nihilism. It is not surprising. Sexuality is the root of all ethics, all politics, no doubt all religion as well."

"Blasphemy!" I fairly shouted.

He fixed me with his eyes, then turned to Le Rennet. "I have nothing more to say."

"Please, you must excuse my companion. He has recently arrived from America. Another continent, an ocean away. The journey is a long one, not simply of space, but of the mind as well. Surely you can understand that, Doctor."

Krafft-Ebing chose to continue, now addressing Le Rennet as if the latter were one among an audience of students. "Societies, like individuals, advance and develop on the basis of their integrated sexuality. The Crown Prince failed in this task of integration. He proceeded from extreme to extreme. Two opposing theses, if you will, but no synthesis. He began early with abnormal sexual impressionability. Later, when I treated him, he suffered from some undiagnosed form of hysterical anesthesia. His sexual life seemed to all but disappear. Normally one encounters this symptom only in children and in senile patients."

"You treated him for impotency, then?"

"Yes, in part. But in reality that complaint only manifested itself intermittently. His body suffered from the demands he had made upon it. Not only sexual demands, which at times seemed bestial, but others. He resorted to alcohol in excess. And the hypodermic. He swung between two poles: insatiability and impotency. Out of this grew a paranoia, a systematized delusion. On occasion, for example when he noted the duty of women to give themselves to him, he seemed messianic. But, as I said, his will dissolved when his past excesses overtook him. He had been receiving treatment for an inflammation of the peritoneum, presumably brought on from exposure during a hunting expedition some years previous. That, of course, was nonsense."

"Yes, Doctor?" prodded Le Rennet. "The complaint was venereal?"

"It was. A persistent gonorrheal infection. The Crown Prince had also transmitted the disease to his wife, Princess Stephanie. When I was called in, the infection had already spread to her ovaries. I could do nothing. She was sterile."

"My God," I breathed.

"But you treated Prince Rudolph?"

"I prescribed sodium salicylate powder, a diuretic tea, morphia suppositories in cocoa butter, Copaiva balsam capsules, and a zinc sulfate ointment. It was the most I could do. Whether it was enough I do not know. I was never asked to return. Instead, I was sworn to secrecy. Until now, I have kept that oath."

"You know nothing more about Rudolph?"

"I recommended baths and hydrotherapy. I heard he travelled to several spas. Not only is the process soothing, but it also has a beneficial effect on suggestible patients. A tour of the waters becomes for many a symbolic baptism, a rebirth. If it so affected Rudolph, I do not know. From his behavior at the last, I doubt it."

"*At the last?*" Le Rennet pounced on the phrase. "Was he driven to take his own life?"

"I am a doctor, not a clairvoyant. Moreover, any knowledge I have of the tragedy comes from newspapers."

"But you do have personal knowledge of Rudolph, of his past behavior. Given his condition, would it have been possible for him to engage in a romantic suicide pact with a young girl he had known for so short a time?"

"If you have read my book, you know that almost anything is possible," the Doctor snapped, as if exasperated with an oafish student. "But to predict what any one man will do or to say with certainty that he has taken a particular action at a particular moment because of conditions and tendencies previously observed—either is foolish. Science has not progressed to such a state, at least not neuropathology."

"Granting the possibility of such an action by Prince Rudolph, or any man for that matter, would it be probable? Would Rudolph, having exhausted himself mentally and physically, reach for his pistol like a ruined gambler?"

Krafft-Ebing was clearly angered at being pressed into an answer. "I will say only that it is not improbable," he finally replied, again biting off each word. "And since you wish to know all, let me give you an item which is *not* a matter of speculation. Rudolph suffered from a repeated formation of Gordeola, perhaps resulting from the spread of the venereal infection. In any case, he suffered continually from sties. I prescribed a yellow mercury ointment and a zinc sulphate solution administered by drops. Now I believe I have fulfilled my obligation."

"You have, Doctor. I am grateful for your candor."

"The thanks are due Her Majesty." He placed his papers in a small case and strode away.

"My God. All that. The Crown Prince of the Empire!"

"Beggars and kings," said Le Rennet. "Beggars and kings."

Need I explain my uneasiness upon our return? I was tired but knew that I would not be able to sleep. I fretted, not knowing how to occupy myself. Fortunately the old man demanded that I dispatch a note to Evans. The message concerned personal names, and to avoid confusion it was Le Rennet's habit not to cipher names in the first instance of their use. His alternate ruse was simple enough. He would have me begin the letter, which was simply a list of names, with three chosen for their number of letters and having no relevance beyond that whatsoever. The dentist would add the total letters, subtract the square root of that total and count that number down from the top of the list, beginning with the fourth name. That was the first name of importance. The process was repeated if there happened to be three or more names following. This time, he was inquiring about Count Samuel Teleki, Johann Salvator, and Moriz Szeps.

In the middle of this task, I recalled one of Evans' earlier messages and immediately sought out Le Rennet in his room. "The page that was missing from the pharmacy book at the Hofburg!" I exclaimed.

"Yes?" Le Rennet did not look up from the photographs of Rudolph which covered his bed. "Did you observe, Griswold, that the Baroness adamantly rejected depression as the cause of Rudolph's demise? She was even more insistent that he would not have committed suicide out of love for Mary Vetsera. On the other hand, she offered no explanation for the Prince's death."

"The page," I repeated impatiently. "If there is any truth in what Krafft-Ebing said of the Prince and the prescriptions he issued, well, that's why the page was removed. To avoid scandal. To hide what was there."

"Or to hide what was not there," the old one said. I made nothing of that. My own deduction seemed a perfect example of ratiocination. Somewhat despondent, I completed the message and set off to the post-box.

Any touch of low spirits disappeared when I opened our front door to the lilt of Mery Laurent's voice. She greeted me fondly, and I joined her and Le Rennet in a glass of wine. Almost at once, however, I was reduced to utter dismay. Le Rennet was entertaining Mery with the sexual theories of Krafft-Ebing. "Sir," I objected, trying to call the man to himself, "you must show respect for fair womankind. It is outside the bounds of all propriety to introduce such lurid subjects—"

"But, Wilmot, I am very interested." Mery shifted her position upon the couch, and I noted that beneath her petticoats she wore a new pair of shoes. They were black patent with an alluring flap over the instep. I stared, embarrassed, and finally said, "What a lovely pair of shoes." She swung a leg higher and mockingly bowed her head. "Why, thank you, Wilmot. I did not know you noticed."

"Beggars and kings," Le Rennet chortled. Damn all. The evening was ruined. With my second glass of wine, I became acutely aware I had not eaten since breakfast. My stomach churned, my head felt unsteady. Worst of all, Krafft-Ebing and his infernal ideas disturbed me, prevented me from enjoying Mery's company. Damn the man, it was as though I had been ordered from Eden.

CHAPTER

6

> ... *while*
> *I pondered, weak and weary,*
> *Over many a quaint and curious*
> *volume of forgotten lore—*

"Sexual instinct—whether experienced as deep emotion or an impulse—is a function of the cerebral cortex. The brain, Griswold, the brain! Hence anything may be *thought* of and produce sexual excitement. Mery Laurent? Of course. But also a political idea, a memory, even a befouled shoe. Anything."

"You are having me, sir! Such ideas are"—not finding a word, I repeated what I had said yesterday—"unnatural!"

"Nonsense. You have been diddled by Rousseau and his noble savages," the old man continued. "Not until man has stepped upon the highest pinnacle of civilization will his *natural* state be reached."

"Aha! You are caught. If what you hold is true, the debauches so dear to Krafft-Ebing make a grotesquerie of all that is noble in man and make impossible his reaching that pinnacle."

"On the contrary, Master Griswold, debauchery is often a

prologue to sainthood. As Charles put it, excesses of all sorts can serve as a mnemonic device. In the depths of degradation, one may glimpse the forgotten ideal. I have had some personal experience in such matters and can testify to the accuracy of Charles' observation. But Rudolph, now. Was his idealism of the sort which would drive him from the world or lock him in endless combat with it? We must uncover more."

"It would seem that Krafft-Ebing left but little to bare," I objected.

"Only part of Rudolph was revealed to the Doctor. We must now concern ourselves with his interior phrenology, the shape of his mind."

So we argued for that day and another, having nothing of significance with which to occupy ourselves. There was only one communication from Evans, to the effect that upon the night of Rudolph's death, Moriz Szeps was in Vienna; Count Samuel Teleki was still exploring Africa, where he had been for three years; and Archduke Johann Salvator was in Fiume. Although the news satisfied Le Rennet, I could see nothing of import and said so. "Consult a map," was his sole comment.

News of a personal nature was dropped almost literally upon my plate that night. Mery, Le Rennet, and I had just consumed an unusually hearty dinner when, after the second bottle of Lafite, she announced she would be leaving Paris. Some ancient dowager had decided to make a party out of opening and airing her summer establishment. Mery had been invited. I suggested I visit her, but she sternly reminded me of my promise to look after the old man. "Besides," she enthused, "you will be in Paris, and Paris is unique upon all the earth at this moment." She gestured about her and spoke at length commending the City's beautiful women, matchless theaters, cafes with their dazzling conversations, the artists and philosophers. "Genius falls about you like spring rain, Wilmot. How wonderful to be living in *la belle epoque*."

I, too, felt it wonderful to be living in this period, but considered its genius to be expressed in commerce, industry, and invention. Frequently what she found exciting seemed to me a matter of sensationalism. As we left the restaurant, we were treated to an example. There, before the eyes of all, in the boulevard's carriage lane, was a dandified man in a derby and striped red and white suit, riding a *bicycle!*

"How *bizarre!*" I exclaimed.

"How delicious," cooed Mery. I suggested that we two walk together for a ways. "In Paris, one does not walk, one dances," she admonished. She pecked me upon the cheek and danced off into the night.

Disheartened by her departing Paris and afflicted with unwholesome imaginings—brought on, I fear, by Krafft-Ebing—I found it necessary, for the next several days, to take laudanum in order to sleep. I was relieved, therefore, to be distracted by the appearance of Baroness Ida Illyes Metzengerstein. Her severe, tailored frock coat and striped trousers contrasted sharply with her effervescence. "It is arranged," she said gleefully, handing me another bottle of brandy. "The Baron will receive you tomorrow morning at ten so that you may begin perusing Rudolph's papers. He sent me to inform you personally and slyly suggested I bring the bottle as a gift. How very like him."

I lit her inevitable cigar, which she drew upon intently until her lips puckered like those of a prissy old maid. "There is more," she said, emptying a pocket. "From Her Majesty. They are letters Rudolph wrote to her. She almost destroyed them, but decided you might find them useful. She asks that you return them to her at a later time. At the moment, she cannot bear the sight of them."

Le Rennet accepted the packet, untied the thin red ribbon, unfolded the sheets of rich paper for us to see. "But they are not in English," I said. "Certainly not," snapped Ida Illyes. "Elisabeth and Rudolph always corresponded in Hungarian. It was she who insisted he learn our language. When Hyazinth

Ronay was pardoned, she immediately brought him to Vienna and engaged him to tutor Rudolph."

"Pardoned?" asked Le Rennet, sorting the letters.

"Yes. In 1848, he sided with the revolutionaries, and when Hungary fell, he went into exile. Franz Joseph pardoned all of them when he assumed the crown of Hungary."

"You will help, Baroness?" Le Rennet held out a letter.

"That is why I am here."

Our work began. Ida Illyes would translate a letter and I would copy as quickly as possible those portions which Le Rennet deemed of moment. Rudolph's letters covered a decade or more, as near as I could make out and were written to his mother during her travels. The travels themselves were dizzying to contemplate.

To Ireland: *I am of course pleased that your mastiff has recovered from the colic. And that you have a fine string of horses at your disposal. But Most Gracious Mother, have you no other thought but sport?*

To Athens: *How marvelous that your enthusiasm for things Greek is rewarded. To be close to Troy seems to affect you like a tonic. Last night we had a dinner to celebrate Vicki's engagement. You were missed greatly. Baron Rothschild was there, and some of the less vulgar of the aristocracy. Why are you always away from me when I most need you?*

To Pest: *It is indeed a question. Is Buda or Pest the more beautiful city? Do they still talk of Stefan Kegl? When I was in Pest last May to review our Regiment, he shot himself. The papers were full of it.*

"Another suicide?" I asked.

"Bah!" retorted Ida Illyes. "Amongst the aristocracy and the better class of people suicide is quite common."

Despite the assurances of Doctor Krafft-Ebing, the subject of a family taint seemed to preoccupy the thoughts of both Elisabeth and Rudolph. When the Empress was recovering from some mysterious malaise by taking the waters at Baden-Baden, he chided her: *Your small wolf with green glimmering eyes is angry. Why must you always dwell upon the house of Wittelsbach? Your cousin Ludwig is dead and best forgotten—how can anyone imagine suicide by simply walking into a lake? He was pursued, trying to escape. And poor Otto, another cousin of misfortune and yourself. He is confined for his own safety. Please do not mention them. You know my fears. Once you even said you shared them!*

Ireland again, and more chiding: *Of course Stephanie and I are not close. Not at all. Why do you keep asking when you already know that? There is but one solution, and you know perfectly well that neither His Majesty nor those tyrants of Rome will hear of it! Enough.*

The Emperor himself was the subject of frequent exchanges, many of bittersweet poignancy. To the island of Corfu: *I am pleased beyond words that you are in health again. When the bloom is in your cheeks, you are the most beautiful woman I know. How is the Emperor, you ask. Alas. He has no friend but that Schratt woman.*

Old Le Rennet paused, holding up his hand in an unspoken question. "Katrina Schratt," explained Ida Illyes impatiently. "His mistress."

"Her Majesty knows?" I asked in disbelief.

"But of course," said the Baroness. "Elisabeth practically arranged it herself so she might be free to travel, to lead her own life without worrying about Franz Joseph."

"My, my," I said. The Baroness ignored me and resumed translating: *The Emperor knows little about the true views and opinions of his people. He believes we are now in one of Austria's happiest eras. Everyone around him tells him so officially. He reads it in the clippings from the newspapers which are daily presented, marked in red, for his perusal. Once, His Majesty was more or less reconciled to the nineteenth century. Now he is again harsh, suspicious, as he used to be in the time of poor Grandma. Time is running short. The Emperor will not change, nor will he abdicate. He is heading for decline and with him, Austria.*

Your Most Gracious Majesty is of course correct on one point: we seem to be living in a midsummer night's dream, and we are indeed forever caressing the ass's head of our illusions.

Rudolph replied to a letter Elisabeth had written from London: *So you visited Madame Tussaud's! And you were fascinated yet repelled by our Emperor's wax figure. I can sympathize, believe me. My esteemed Father has the same effect upon me at our every meeting. What must the people think as they walk by his stiff formal figure, believing him the leader of Europe? Do not give away any more of your jewelry to beggars! You know how strict His Majesty is about finances. When will you abandon your restless way of life and come home? The Court is empty without you, you must know that.*

A month later, again to London, he wrote: *I know, I know. Life is dull in Vienna. But why must my Most Gracious Mother cling to the whistling mane of every wind? (Did you really laugh in the face of Victoria's minister, as rumor has it?) We, both of us, need you. I will readily acknowledge that here in Vienna one finds crookedness, thievery, brutality, arbitrariness, corruption, weakness of the state, and unimaginable boredom for Her Highness. The most important positions are filled by riffraff which you would of necessity be thrown among at court. But how long before such an old and solid building as Austria will collapse? I can do nothing. I am waiting, eternally waiting, to do somethings. All I receive are continuous slights. If you were here, could you not use your influence with His Majesty? To convince him that I must have something to do, something of significance? Please!*

To Heidelberg: *You are closer now than you have been in months. Why do you not come home? Each morning I awake and find myself in prison. I can see the chains that bind my hands, but can do nothing to break them. Did you receive the Heine manuscript I sent you? The four poems are in his*

116

own hand, and are quite moving in their sentiment. Are you still writing? Do send me your thoughts.

Once more to Corfu: *So! Despite our troubles with Turkey, you insisted upon taking the* Miramar *to Smyrna. How shall I greet Frau Freifalik? Really, to costume your hairdresser as yourself and send her sailing up and down the harbor while you, dressed as a peasant, go shopping. Just like that time on the Riviera when she wore your bathing dress and was mobbed by the crowds while you and Elise sat on the balcony, ignored. And free, you will add. I have received word of you—not FROM you!—through our ambassadors in Rhodes, Cyprus, and Port Said. Will you now sail to Godollo and wait? For what?*

"A moment," said Ida Illyes, again experiencing difficulty with Rudolph's handwriting. "Yes, that is the word: *Nimbus.*" *My Emperor will not let me forget his nimbus. Nothing has changed. The mask of civilization will melt like wax if we do not have the courage and the will to proceed—*"There seems to be a page missing. It ends abruptly:" *There is a sinister silence here, like the silence before a thunderstorm. I must . . .* "That is all, there is a page missing."

She drained her brandy and suggested we leave off. Her eyes were troubling her, from the smoke no doubt, as well as from the task of reading the Crown Prince's scratchy hand. Also, it seemed to me at least, Rudolph's letters had moved her. "Tomorrow or the next day, perhaps we can continue." Her mien uncommonly subdued, the Baroness left.

While Le Rennet spread the letters on the table, I quickly ordered my thoughts. "Yes, it could have happened that way. The Prince was frustrated in his attempts to play an active role in his country's governance. He was ignored by his father, deserted by his mother. I find it difficult to believe, and sad, that the *Most Gracious Highness* and the *Emperor* of his letters were actually his own mother and father. A lonely man, Prince—or no. Lonely but jaded by excesses and suddenly enamored of Mary Vetsera, a new and youthful love.

An impossible love. I see them as a pair of star-crossed lovers who perhaps acted out in their lives the very plot of the Immortal Bard—"

"Shut up, Griswold," Le Rennet said softly, studying the letters. It was some time before he said, "You offer a pleasant explanation for a complex problem. But like many pleasant things, it is more pleasant than true. Here, for instance, look at these." He handed me a batch of letters. I objected. "I cannot read Hungarian, as you most certainly know."

"I am not suggesting that you read them, Master Griswold. Just look at them." I did as he instructed, heard him pour another tot of brandy into our glasses. "Well?" he demanded.

I returned the letters to him with a shrug. "What am I to see?"

"The calligraphy. Did you not notice how it changes, how it seems to deteriorate?"

"May I see them again?" This time I placed them across the table top and stood up to review them. "Yes, there is a change. These later letters are crudely written, sloppily scrawled. The lines no longer march uniformly across the page. But how is that inconsistent with what I said? He was desperate. Besides," I added triumphantly, "Krafft-Ebing— recall what he told us? The Prince had trouble with his eyes. Put that together with his desperation and we see how Rudolph's handwriting presents a perfect picture of a man breaking under profound pressure."

"You are correct, Master Griswold. It is perfect." He finished his brandy and suggested we take an early dinner at one of his favorite disreputable cafes.

In preparation for his survey of Prince Rudolph's books and memoirs, "to discover the very shape of his mind" as Le Rennet put it, the old man was thoroughness itself. He roused me at dawn and, as soon as the shops were open, propelled me out the door. We purchased a *cahier*, or copybook, for me to take notes in, as well as a reading glass with which he might ease the strain on his eyes. Since the material presumably would be in the Prince's native language, we also obtained a small German dictionary. At still another shop, the old man purchased six sets of linen, new shirts, collars and cuffs of the latest fashion. I remarked upon this odd expenditure, but he simply replied that one must be prepared for the Baron.

When we arrived shortly after ten, we were greeted by Baron Metzengerstein himself and led down the corridor of shameful art to the room where Le Rennet had played that astonishing hand of whist. If the Baron retained any rancor he certainly did not show it. At least, not to the old man. However, he did nod to a bottle of brandy and apologize to me. "I am sorry, M. Griswold. This is excellent, but not the best. My stock of the latter has recently been . . . depleted." Without a pause he moved to some shipping boxes which were then opened for us. As an aide we were given a graying, bespectacled old man who was introduced as a minor secretary from the Austrian Embassy. "He will assist you in any way possible," the Baron said to Le Rennet.

"You are most kind."

"My pleasure. But there is just one small point. I have drawn a . . . protocol, officially attesting that I have complied with instructions given me. Would you be so gracious as to sign, please? Three copies. To avoid any misunderstanding, I have composed it in English." Although the Baron spoke only to Le Rennet, my curiosity got the better of my discretion and I examined one of the copies. At the head of the crisp white sheet was the black Austrian double eagle with the embossed seal of the Paris Embassy. The message itself was brief, written on one of those new writing machines:

1.4.89

The Ministry of the Imperial Household

For information

Prepared by Frederick, Baron von Metzengerstein and signed in his Presence.

I, the undersigned, do depose and swear that I have been allowed full and free access to the papers, journals, memoranda, and other materia literaria of the late His Highness Crown Prince Rudolph.

M. Henri Le Rennet

As Le Rennet signed, I became qualmish. The date, April the first. Was the Baron to make April Fish of us? "Most satisfactory," he said, smiling brightly. "And now you must excuse me and the Baroness. There is a function we must attend. Should you desire anything, simply ask Wilhelm and it shall be yours." His hand resting lightly on the door, Metzengerstein bowed to us before gently closing it behind him.

Wilhelm was so quiet, so self-effacing, that one at times forgot his presence. Diffidently he explained that he had labored for years in Austria's archives and thus was conversant with the material at hand. "Here, gentlemen, is the Crown Prince project." The crate was jammed with twenty-four volumes. "*The Austro-Hungarian Monarchy in Words and Pictures,*" Wilhelm translated. Since this was but one crate of many and since the volumes were printed in German, I was overwhelmed with the spectre of months—nay, years!—spent working through them. Our cicerone next displayed the contents of several boxes, the "youthful writings" of the Crown Prince, those done before his eighteenth birthday when his formal education ended. These classroom essays seemed of scant value, but the old man, as usual full of surprises, thumbed through this collection for nearly an hour, occasionally asking a casual question of Wilhelm. When I queried the usefulness of his browsing, he quoted a verse:

'Tis education forms the common mind;
Just as the twig is bent, the tree's inclined.

"But naturally Rudolph did not have a common mind," said the ever-present Wilhelm.

"I can believe that, sir," said Le Rennet. "Indeed if he had, I would not be troubling you."

Rudolph, it seemed, was as avid a traveller as his Royal Mother and had written extensively of his journeys. Le Rennet seized one such volume and greedily scrutinized it. "Yes, yes. This must be it."

The "it" was a volume in German entitled, Wilhelm explained, *Fifteen Days Upon the Danube.* Written by Rudolph in 1879, it was extremely popular. Wilhelm was as puzzled as I when Le Rennet excitedly paged through the volume and, reading glass in hand, noted passages which I was to translate and record in my notebook. Necessarily, the dictionary and Wilhelm were in constant use since I had no real knowledge of the language. Le Rennet paced, growing irritable with our slowness. Randomly he picked up odd pieces of Rudolph's writings. In so far as I could tell—bent as I was to the task at hand—he rarely used his reading glass. Most often he impatiently thrust the work aside, jerking now and again at his new cuffs. Once he sat down and demanded that I read aloud what I had thus far written. "Good. But you must continue."

He renewed his fitful peregrination, but this time he frequently interrupted us, asking Wilhelm to identify or to summarize memoranda written by Rudolph to various government agencies, involving such items as the opening of parks and railways, the celebration of annual civic events. Just as I was about to remonstrate with him for so delaying us, he abruptly announced that he was fatigued and ordered me to note my place in the translation so that I might continue on the morrow. Elaborately he thanked Wilhelm. "You will be welcome at any time," the latter responded somewhat wanly.

"Absurd, sir," I said to Le Rennet when we had seated ourselves at a cafe and ordered a brandy. "Hours have been wasted. For what?" Piqued, I pushed my copy-book towards him. "A graceless translation, even at points confused. I do not know how you can expect to make sense of it." Le Rennet took the copy-book, studied it, asked questions about certain portions; then, tucking it under his arm, he arose and simply walked away. I was left to pay *l'addition*.

When I overtook him, he was whistling happily. "That should convince them," he said.

"Whom?"

"The Baron. Wilhelm. The man who followed us from the Baron's mansion to the cafe and who is escorting us home."

"I see no one unusual," I said, looking behind us.

"Excellent, Master Griswold. Just the right touch of furtiveness. The big man, lumbering under a seaman's trunk. You last saw him at the Baron's, in livery." Before I could look again, Le Rennet hailed a hack and we sped off into the dusk.

Upon arriving at our wreck of an abode—such a contrast to the Baron's sumptuous residence—I suggested we have a meal since we had eaten nothing since breakfast. Le Rennet would have none of it. "We have work to do before the words become cold and my mind fails me."

"You talk in riddles, sir. Why, just a short while ago, you seemed satisfied with my work, as poor as it might be. Surely Rudolph's account of a trip up the Danube will wait upon some cold beef and a glass of wine!"

"The Danube!" Le Rennet spoke contemptuously. "That is patriotic drivel, for popular consumption. A Strauss waltz of travel."

"Then why in heaven's name did you insist I spend hours on it?"

"So that I would be free to accomplish this." He removed his coat and gestured at his shirt cuffs. "Wilhelm was a spy, of course," he added nonchalantly as he removed the stiff cuffs and handed them to me. They were covered with tiny penciled scribblings which seemed little more than specks of ash.

"What does all this mean?" I asked.

"It is a system of abbreviated writing, which explains my haste. I must not forget so much that I cannot transcribe the words. And I am afraid you must do yet more copy work." He waved me to the table where pen, ink, and paper still remained from yesterday's translation of Rudolph's letters. He did, however, bring us both some wine before he picked up his magnifying glass and began reading aloud from his cuffs.

The clergy did most harm by understanding how to make the people humble and submissive through superstition and exaggerated piety, so that they and the nobility had an easy task and were able to do with the poor people whatever they wished.

Kingship now is like a mighty ruin which remains from to-day to tomorrow but must eventually sink into the ground. For hundreds of years it survived, and for as long as the people allowed themselves to be led blindly it was good—but now its task is finished, men are free, and at the next storm the ruin will sink.

"You are telling me, sir, that Rudolph, a future monarch, wrote those words? It does not sound altogether like his letters. And certainly this is not the Rudolph that Krafft-Ebing described."

"The same. These passages are from a paper he presented to his tutor entitled *Random Thoughts*. Listen to this:" *Ideas of all kinds drift through my mind, my head is a turmoil, and my brain is seething and working all day long; no sooner has one idea left than another enters; each one of them occupies me, each one of them tells me something different; cheerful and gay, at one moment, raven-black at the next, or full of fury.*

"*Turmoil. Seething.* Now that sounds more like the Doctor's Prince."

"You forget, Griswold, that Rudolph was considerably younger when he wrote these words. But you have missed the point again. In all his serious writings, the Prince exhibited an inquiring and receptive mind. He was alive with ideas. Indeed, the *turmoil* belonged not so much to him as to our times. He absorbed it and the ideas at its heart. He became their advocate. Copy this carefully:" *The principle of nationalism is based on common animal instincts. It is essentially the victory of fleshly sympathies and instincts over spiritual and cultural ideas. I consider all enmity based on nationality or race a great retrogression.*

"A truly noble sentiment, one which would do honor to his position as a ruler of a large empire."

"Perhaps. But consider this passage:" *The church in Austria must be stripped of its holdings, aristocrats taxed suitably, land distributed, estates parcelled out among the peasantry.* "And this:" *There will be wars until the people and the nations have completed their development, until they at last unite themselves and mankind has become one great family.*

I paused to flex my fingers, choosing to comment only on the last sentence. "A generous view of mankind."

"Now listen to this, Griswold, written shortly before he died." *Dark and ugly times await us. One can almost believe that old Europe is outdated and beginning to disintegrate. A great and thorough reaction has to set in, a social upheaval from which, after a long illness, a wholly new Europe may blossom.* "Then comes:" *Every year I grow older, that is, less vital and less able. This eternal period of preparing yourself, this continuous waiting for the time when construction can begin, saps my creative energy.* "And later:" *I am disgusted. So close to the hub of political life but with no chance of intervening in it. What can I do?* "Still later:" *From day to day I observe more clearly with how narrow a circle of spies, of denunciation and watchfulness, I am surrounded.* "Is this a mind, Griswold, which would wallow in self-pity, which would fall under the spell of a pretty face and end its struggle?

"Well," I offered, "his ideas are, without doubt, progressive. Such a person, internally rent, skeptical, without the anchor of religion . . ."

"His ideas are not merely progressive. Mark me, they are prophetic."

"And a prophet is without honor in his own land."

Le Rennet's jaw slackened. He stared at me. "At times, Master Griswold, you amaze me."

The source of an unholy clamor at our door proved to be Baroness Metzengerstein. I was embraced but received no brandy. "How wise you were not to trust Wilhelm. When I left, he and the Baron were having a celebratory drink, both entertained by your copying from Rudolph's frivolous notes on the Danube. Yet I must warn you. Freddy is of a suspecting nature. Though he laughed, I knew that he had not forgotten our game of whist, M. Le Rennet. Here, you must have this," she continued, giving the old one a volume the size of a pamphlet. "Naturally, they left out many of Rudolph's papers and writings. When he was in England some ten years ago, he published this book anonymously, at his own expense. Everyone knew who had written it, but, unlike Salvator, Rudolph did not acknowledge his authorship."

"Archduke Salvator?" asked Le Rennet. "What did he publish?"

"A scandalous piece, highly critical of the Austrian military, especially the artillery. Called them ill-trained, loutish buffoons. Since Salvator was an officer in the Austrian artillery, the Emperor was incensed. For him, Salvator was a threat to the discipline and order which held the Empire together. So Salvator was reprimanded and transferred to an obscure infantry regiment. He should never have declared himself the author."

I enthusiastically scanned the volume which Le Rennet handed me before he poured Ida Illyes some wine. It was in English! No more fiddling with verbs and such. The title, I must say, was regal enough: *The Austrian Aristocracy and Its Constitutional Vocation: An Admonition to the Aristocratic Youth from an Austrian.* According to the Crown Prince, if indeed this were his work, the aristocracy of Austria was behaving irresponsibly, sowing the seeds of the Empire's destruction. The young aristocrats, particularly, were concerned only with crude language and horses. " 'A festering sore upon the body politic,' " I read aloud.

Le Rennet repeated the phrase. "I like that. It parallels certain thoughts óf my own. I wonder, Baroness, how would Rudolph have treated this wound? Cleansing? Bleeding? Excision?"

"Whatever he would have done, it would have been . . ." She lacked a word.

"Drastic," I supplied.

"Permanent," she retorted. "Rudolph was a visionary dedicated to a future without such louts in positions of authority. Come," she crooked a finger at me, "we must go."

"Where?"

"Remember, the Baron thinks I am enamored of you," she whistled in imitation of my unfortunate impediment. "We shall go to a cafe or two. Followed, of course. He will be satisfied."

Our destination was a warehouse which had been converted into a cafe by pushing piles of refuse into the corners and adding two dozen tables with ill-matching, uncomfortable chairs. The waiters were dressed in spattered academic regalia: mortar boards and black gowns. Their typical French surliness waxed into effrontery. The customers, from some perversity, delighted in it. And as God is my judge, there, wandering about the room, was a full-grown donkey called The Professor. He consumed unattended drinks, was fed scraps of fried bread, and, to the applause of the patrons, urinated upon the floor. Ida Illyes ordered cigars and absinthe —a drink I had determined to avoid but which I found quite tasty. I recall sipping it while the Baroness exchanged shouts with a young man—I think it was a young man—across the room. Unfortunately, little else of that night comes to mind except a distorted picture of Ida Illyes leaning from a cab, brazenly whistling, and the sound of Le Rennet's laughter crashing through my head.

CHAPTER

7

He who has never swooned is not he who
beholds floating in mid-air the sad
visions that the many may not view.

"*Wolkenkraxler*. YES," SAID WILHELM, "THAT DOES MEAN
'a cloud climber, a builder of cloud castles, a visionary.' "

"An appropriate expression," I said dully, closing the
dictionary. My last night's wanderings with the Baroness had
left me with a dry mouth, an aching head, and a waspish
temper. I had flatly refused when Le Rennet insisted I continue the useless exercise of copying pretty phrases about
the Danube. "Enough, sir," I had said, swigging down one of
his tomato concoctions. He had relented and, upon arrival at
the Baron's, presented me with a lengthy memorandum which
the Crown Prince had sent to Emperor Franz Joseph, an
analysis of current political conditions in Austria-Hungary.
But what particularly interested Le Rennet was the hand-
written note accompanying the memorandum: *Will the Em-*
peror take this, my small work, seriously, or will he leaf
through it before falling asleep and file it among the other
documents, considering it a piece of eccentricity to be ex-
pected from and cut in the pattern of a cloud climber?

Having dutifully copied the note, I now began on the memorandum itself. I had no enthusiasm, not only because of my weakened physical state but also because the undertaking might be just another one of the old man's ruses. As the morning wore on, I grew increasingly sympathetic to Rudolph's railing against senseless tasks. Even Wilhelm's attention wandered.

I was delighted, therefore, when the Baron himself interrupted us with an invitation to join him for a midday meal. He overruled Le Rennet's demur, saying: "It is a light repast, which we may enjoy without formality, as befits men who labor long and hard."

No formality! A light repast! The chamber to which he led us was bathed in light from exquisite chandeliers, the light itself reflected in glasses, goblets, china and silver. Liveried servants were stationed at sideboards which groaned under fowl, beef, lobster, and countless covered dishes. I felt as if I had magically entered a scene from my youthful musings on the courtly life, a sensation which was heightened by the golden flow of champagne and the soft music from a viola and pianoforte. Ida Illyes, dressed in a brown cheviot suit and a sateen shirt, smoking her cigars, did not disturb the fantasy but unaccountably contributed to it. If anything marred the interlude it was Le Rennet who ate little and maintained a curious silence, responding not at all to the Baron's amusing anecdotes and skillful *repartee* with the Baroness.

At meal's end, the Baron suddenly pulled me aside and led me to a curtained painting on the wall above a sideboard. At a word from him, the foodstuffs and the piece of furniture were removed. The Baron dramatically pulled a cord, the curtains parted, and I gazed, paralyzed and speechless. "It is a masterpiece, is it not? A Manet, of his later period." Still I could not speak or move. The subject of the painting was Mery Laurent, fully, most revealingly, nude. "I knew you would enjoy it," said the Baron. Two settees were placed beneath the portrait, coffee and brandy were poured. I kept my eyes averted from the lovely Mery. Enchantment had disappeared and I felt somehow ashamed. That she should be revealed—no, displayed—to me in such a fashion was wrong.

I realized, after some moments, that the Baron had begun speaking of Rudolph. "Did you know, M. Le Rennet, that the Crown Prince died . . . not in poverty, of course . . . but deeply in debt? To be frank, at this point no one is certain quite how deeply in debt he was."

"Surely that is unusual for an heir to the throne," I proffered, making an effort at civil conversation.

"Such a state of affairs is not unusual, but then neither, I suppose, is it usual."

"Oh," I said, feeling myself rebuffed.

"But in Rudolph's case it was extreme. The Empress Maria Theresa secured the Hapsburg fortune in an extraordinary manner."

"I have studied her statue," said Ida Illyes. "She had a beautiful Hungarian face."

"As may be. She was also quite shrewd in matters of finance. The personal fortune of the Hapsburgs remains in a trust established by Maria Theresa and administered by the Emperor himself. This trust, of course, is also part of the . . . shall we say *assets*? . . . of the Empire. As you can imagine, the distinction between personal and state monies is complex. At times, expenditures are actually indistinguishable."

I was confused, but Le Rennet said, "I believe I understand."

"Good. Now, then. There is this Jew who lives on the rue . . ."

"Rue du Faubourg," said Le Rennet testily.

"Yes. A Galician Jew," the Baron hissed, his eyes narrowing above his puffy cheeks, thus emphasizing his porcine appearance. "He is a goldsmith, he claims, and a dealer in precious jewellery. He is also suspected of receiving, from time to time, stolen goods. He was discovered to have two rings in his possession. Unusual rings. One, in particular, should interest you. Beneath the diamond, stamped in the setting, is the Great Seal of Austria. On the band is an inscription from His Majesty Franz Joseph to his wife. There can be no doubt of the ring's origin or rightful owner."

"No!" shouted Ida Illyes, suddenly erect, eyes blazing.

"I have no choice. I must perform my duty. That ring is a part of the Austrian people's heritage. The Jew claims he legally purchased it from an old man last February. His documents have been examined and found to be in order. The name of the seller is quite plain: Henri Le Rennet. The signature matches the one on the protocol, M. Le Rennet—in all points."

"You can't!" pleaded Ida Illyes.

"I have reported the theft. I could do nothing else. Perhaps, in time, the matter will clear itself up. Until then . . ." He waved toward a door which a servant opened. In strode four *gendarmes,* one with a weapon drawn. He addressed my aged friend in clipped English. "You will be pleased to accompany us." Another *gendarme* nodded at me and looked questioningly at the Baron.

"He is innocent," said Le Rennet firmly.

"I wonder," came that chilling voice. "Is he, Baroness? Take him too." As we were shoved from the room, the Baron laughed and called out, "Halt!" He approached Le Rennet. "We were discussing the Empress Maria Theresa. Her Majesty was an accomplished woman, given to composing aphorisms. Here is one you might ponder . . . in your free time. 'Those who are born in boots should not desire to wear shoes.' *Adieu.*"

"This is unthinkable!" I cried as we were pushed into a black carriage, entirely enclosed. *"Taisez-vous!"* shouted a *gendarme,* menacing me with a club. We were thrust onto a narrow wooden bench. The *gendarme* and a companion hulked across from us. The door was locked from the outside. We moved. My spirits teetered violently as we were pitched from side to side in our springless box. Immediately, I wished for the solace of companionship, but communication with Le Rennet would be futile as he indicated by a barely perceptible shake of his head. The next moment, I was thoroughly enraged. Nonetheless, I pressed my hands together. What could I do, unarmed, virtually singlehandedly? Shortly, rage gave way to sense, to the certainty that this horrendous error would be speedily rectified. So I closed my eyes and busied myself with the retribution to be exacted from the Baron, his status be damned.

Yet I could not sustain those visions. The journey was interminable and the air grew intolerably foul. Release was all I could think of. At last it came. Wearily, we climbed down into the courtyard of a forbidding stone structure, only to be hauled before an official of considerable rank, if his braided uniform was any indication. While we stood at a wooden railing, I quietly spoke to Le Rennet. "Surely, we must call for Etienne."

"The Prefect of the Paris police can do little for us. We are not in Paris. On his own, he has no authority here."

"But—"

"*Taisez-vous*! *Finissez*!" shouted the official and I was cuffed on the head by a *gendarme*. The official looked at us with disdain. "I am Chef de Commissariat Lambert. You will speak only when I give permission. You. You are Henri Le Rennet?" The old man nodded and was brutally struck by the *gendarme*. "I asked you a question, Monsieur."

"I am Henri Le Rennet."

"Then sign here," he said, extending a pen. "Good. And you? What is your name?"

"Wilmot Rufus Griswold. A citizen of the United States."

"You are both thieves. Take them away."

I pulled from the grasp of the *gendarme*. "No, sir. This cannot be." I protested our innocence and reminded them of the sacred concepts of liberty, equality, and fraternity amongst all men. I stood upon my rights as an American and demanded to speak to a higher official.

"*Quel fou*," said Lambert. I was struck upon the head.

I am a hearty Baltimorean who prides himself upon courage and manliness. In the establishment of early trade in Bob's Oil I, myself, canvassed a portion of our country's Western frontiers, where dangers are manifold—from man, from beast, from the land itself. As a youngster I experienced violence and bloodshed during the last year of the war to preserve our Union. Yet nothing had prepared me for the terrors which clutched me.

That eternity of torment, of monstrousness, was instantaneously palpable when I awoke. My eyes were open, but to utter darkness. There was a weight upon my breast which made breathing painful. By touch, I determined it was Le Rennet who had apparently been sitting over me and collapsed on my chest. I gained my feet and lowered him to the couch where I had been lying. (Couch? Rough boards covered by lice-ridden straw!) The old man's heart was so weak that I thought it had stopped. With hands made clumsy by desperation, I searched his clothing and recovered four nitrate pearls. I placed one in a handkerchief, crushed it between my fingers and held it beneath his nostrils. He did not move. I crushed a second pearl and waited. He turned his head away, groaning. I felt his heartbeat increase. For the moment, it appeared he would live.

I began to explore our prison. Nay, dungeon! The odor of human waste pervaded and movement was made difficult since the stone floor was treacherous with slime. I was soon lost in that blackness, so, to secure my bearings, I shuffled forward, arms raised in front of me, until I touched a wall. It was stone masonry, smooth, damp, cold. Panic washed over me and I shouted to Le Rennet. No response. I listened intently and at length distinguished three sounds. One was a soft gurgling of water somewhere above. The other two I could not identify but both sounded like breathing. Were there other occupants of our dungeon?

"Is anyone there?" I called out. No answer. I started a circuit of our cell, using the clammy wall as my guide. It was then I noticed ever-so-dim lines which met to form a rectangle. The door. It was locked, of course, but at least it provided a point of reference. As I slowly continued to grope my way along the wall, I discovered metal plates, pins, and chains—instruments of torture and slow death.

A rhythmic rasping sent me to the old man. When he coughed, I was shocked by the suddenness of the sound. I sat beside him, grasped his hands in mine, and began massaging them. If I had wished for the solace of companionship in that rattling carriage, now I absolutely required it. But though he coughed again, he said nothing. I clung to him, my agitation of spirit keeping me awake. Mercifully, however, I did drift off, for I dreamed, and in that dream, I found myself in the brilliance of the Baron's dining hall—what irony!—and Mery Laurent floated above me, just out of reach of my fingertips.

The terror of my next awakening has never been equalled. Aware of some slight movement or change of current in that dank, still air, I started to my feet. Perspiration burst from every pore. In the darkness I could discern phantoms moving in a macabre dance about the door. A shape passed through a sliver of light, then another and another. Rats! The largest I have even seen. A portal opened, about a foot square and at the bottom of the door. A shaft of light fell into our prison to reveal a rat springing forward followed by troops of others. A wooden bowl and an earthen jug were shoved into the room. The portal slammed shut. Flurries and screeches as the rats attacked the bowl, apparently wiping it clean in seconds. Wild, still ravenous, they turned to me and the old man. Cursing, I flailed at them. So it was that I did not at first hear the kicking upon our door. After much shouting, I learned that I was to return the bowl and the jug—the water had been spilled by the rats, of course—through the portal.

Involuntarily squinting against the light, I found myself facing a large square-toed shoe. I put down the impulse to grab it, shake it, tear it—something. I did as ordered.

Thus passed what I later ascertained was our first day of captivity. On the second, the old man regained partial consciousness and began raving. "There, there, I see you!" he screamed, pointing a barely visible arm to a far corner of our cell. He then carried on maniacal conversations with what he described as a beautiful woman whose flowing robes were afire. "I see! I see! Take them away. No more!"

"What shall I take away, sir?" I asked, trying to humor him from his delusion. "The cauldrons, those steaming, fizzling cauldrons. There, in the moonlight. She is going to drown me in boiling liquor. If once I falter, down, down, down she will plunge me to the chin in the burning brandy, there to squirm like Tantalus, with parched throat, starting eyeballs, and agonies of pain. Don't let her do it. Help. Help! O God, help me!"

He lapsed into insensibility and I was left all the more aware of my agonizing thirst. I could hear that gurgling water from above, but I could not reach it. I searched our cell and found only a small open pipe, a sewer for our wastes, I gathered, which emitted a stench that nearly caused me to swoon.

"I see your trap! I recognized the conspirators. Fiends," again the old man ranted. "I am ready for you. For all of you. I shall not falter. I will not!" He fell to babbling, rehearsing the persecution of the man he claimed to be. The upshot was always the same: Edgar Allan Poe had menaced one of the most popular political figures in America and so his demise had been necessary.

"Brandy!" he screamed over and over. His cry seemed to issue not merely from a need for physical relief, from a *mania-a-potu*, as it were. His ramblings, which mingled madness and philosophy of the most *bizarre* sort, were in themselves a plea for release from *moral* horrors. Moreover, the brandy apparently would deaden the pain of a searing inward wound caused by some *aesthetic* perturbation. As his mania worsened, his strength increased and I found it difficult to extract myself from his grasp.

At last I heard the rats returning. By an inward instinct or mechanism, they knew that our food would soon arrive. When I tried to rise, the old man fought to keep me with him.

"No. Don't leave me. You can't leave me." But if we were to survive, I had to. I hit him soundly upon the chin and he fell back onto the straw.

There was no time to spare. Troops of rats swarmed into our cell and, as if they divined my purpose, they attached themselves to my legs. I slipped and fell upon the floor, only to be covered by those appalling creatures. I tossed them from me as best I could and reached a wooden stool. Raising it, I gathered all my remaining strength and waded into the pack. Rats, dead and dying rats, flew about the chamber. They were set upon and devoured by their own kind. An abomination. Yet the loathing which I felt mounting within me was short-lived, for I realized that my path to the door was free. I was ready.

The portal swung open, the bowl and jug were shoved through. It closed. The rats, as if strengthened by a satanic force, renewed their attack on me. They swarmed at my feet, my legs, vainly jumping for the bowl and jug which I had raised above my head. I kicked the stool forward. I felt a claw rake my cheek. But I reached Le Rennet and with my back against the wall, defended our rations. Alternately, I swung the stool and hungrily dipped my fingers into a vile cabbage soup with a few pieces of stale bread floating in it. I tried to stuff some of the mess into Le Rennet's mouth. But he was still unconscious and his choking attracted the rats toward his unprotected face. I desisted and, despite waves of nausea, finished the soup. To dislodge some vicious rodents, I flung the bowl at the door where it was soon covered by a sea of furry greed.

Again I sought to rouse Le Rennet. The water, the precious water. He had to drink or die. A nitrate pearl brought him round briefly. I forced the jug to his lips. "Drink, damn you. Drink!" He sputtered but finally swallowed, gulping the water, yet some of it trickled down his chin. "Enough!" I had to say. I broke from his grasp and consumed the remaining ounces. There was an angry kick upon the door. Hurriedly, I retrieved the bowl and waited at the portal. It swung open and I pushed the dishes outward.

Deprived of their dinner, the rats scavenged for scraps, even those which clung to our lips and fingers. They would not cease their attacks upon us. I flayed my arms, kicked, stomped. Again and again I raised the stool, which ultimately broke as it crashed to the floor. I grew so weary that I slouched next to Le Rennet, weakly waving away the rats from his chest and face. He continued, at times, to break into his ravings. I actually began to look forward to them, not only because they temporarily frightened off the hordes but also because they kept me sane. Though frightful, his voice was still human. Without it, I might have yielded to terror, might also have sunk into some personal hell. And from that hell there would have been no return.

But what boots it to tell in further detail of the long, long hours of horror more than mortal. The days passed. And, blessedly, Le Rennet recovered his reason. He grew able to maneuver, to assist me in securing from the rats sufficient food and drink to survive. He tore a swatch from his shirt; after we drank our allotment of water, the rag was soaked in the liquid and we were able to preserve it for later. We alternated, one eating, the other fending off the vermin. In a word, we established a routine which enabled us to stay alive.

Le Rennet, in fact, became philosophical. "Don't blame the rats, Master Griswold. After all, this is their domain. We are the intruders who are stealing their food, depriving their young of sustenance." He even waxed lyrical about Baron Metzengerstein!

"The actions of the Baron, sir, were infamous. Nothing can excuse them."

"The Baron has his flaws, but failing to perform his duty is not one of them. Perform it he did, and it does not matter that personal considerations acted as additional goads."

"Duty? To imprison two utterly innocent individuals?"

"Yes, duty. He believes that, for the good of the Empire, the door must be closed on Mayerling. Closed, sealed, never more to be opened. In this belief, he is like the man he serves, Count Taaffe. Moreover, Griswold, history has little regard for individuals. And the Empire must continue to make history; servants of other states have thought similarly. No, if I were to criticize the Baron, it would be for knowing more than we do, but suspecting less."

"Well, sir, I am not sure there is more which we must know, or that there is really anything to suspect. From the beginning—"

"The beginning, Griswold? But we shall know, I mean definitely *know*, the beginning only when we have reached the end." My God, I thought, even in a dungeon I am not without Frenchified conceits! I protested.

"All right, Master Griswold, where would you begin?"

"Why, with the suicide—for it seems to me—of Crown Prince Rudolph, of course."

"And then? How do we proceed to understand that event?"

"By looking at the causes. Prince Rudolph's frustration at not achieving an influential position within the government of an Empire he was destined to rule. His estrangement from his mother and father. His unsatisfactory marriage. His hopeless love affair with Mary Vetsera. The internal pressures which rent his personality, the diseased body, the drugged and drunken mind, the unstable emotions of his last years. Surely when these are considered as causes, his suicide is more than understandable. It is obvious."

"In the excellent pursuit of your causes, Master Griswold, you have tended to overlook facts. The fact, for example, that a priest named Degrote was told of Rudolph's death before it was discovered."

"A hoax, sir. Why the name of Vicomte Montreine is not even known amongst European nobility, as you yourself discovered."

"And that is another fact. Then there is Loschek's statement. The Keeper of the Outer Door, the trusted and respected servant of the Prince, he merely glances into the room and declares, 'They are both dead!' "

"I fail to discern how these peripheral matters affect the conclusion that has been drawn."

"It is precisely because they do not fit your pattern, that you must discard them. But suppose there is a different pattern. What was it Charles wrote? A man walks through a forest of symbols and they correspond. Our ratiocinations must be directed toward discovering those correspondences. Do you detect a correspondence between Rudolph's political writings and his deterioration as exemplified by his behavior, his dress, his personal grooming and his handwriting?"

"His disappointment in not carrying his ideals of government into action are thus revealed!" Rankled by his affectation of profundity, I added, "But no doubt you have unearthed a deeper meaning."

"Truth is not always a well; in fact, as regards the more important knowledge, I do believe that she is invariably superficial."

"Meaning?"

"That I do not suggest a 'deeper meaning,' as you put it. Simply a different one. I believe our evening repast is on its way, and it is quite early."

Footsteps sounded, followed by the clanking of keys and the groaning of the door itself, not simply the tiny portal! Unbearable light burst in on us, unbearable but delicious light! I cried out in pain, but also in joy. Rescue had come. Arms grasped Le Rennet and me. We were escorted, half-carried, up flight after flight of stone steps.

We traversed a corridor, proceeded through a door and across the courtyard. Our guards paused while the old man and I breathed fully and frequently of the fresh air. Through partially opened eyes, I espied the late afternoon sun. It danced in the distance, alive! Once, when we passed a gallery window, Mery Laurent had pointed out a painting to me. By Van Gogh. The sun had that quality in the painting as I now experienced. Had the painter also been imprisoned so his eyes were highly attuned to the very vitality of light?

We resumed our walk across the courtyard and arrived at a well-lighted room containing an official in black robes, Alexandre Etienne, and Jared Rathbone!

"You are alive at least. I suppose that's something. There is consternation in high places. The Embassy of the United States is embarrassed. If it weren't for the repeated claims of a Baroness Metzengerstein that two Americans were being held for theft, and if I had not recognized your name, Griswold, you would still be in prison. Locked up. Not that you probably don't belong there. It was only through the Prefecture, Etienne here, that I was able to intercede. You are at liberty. For how long, depends on the French government. The United States has officially washed its hands of the matter."

"I thank you deeply, sir. We both do." As I spoke he looked at me with distaste. No wonder. I still whistled faintly and my recent confinement had lent a certain harshness to my voice. I was unkempt and wretchedly unclean, with wounds from savage rats. Yet if he had undergone even a portion of our experience, I thought, would he not have been more compassionate?

"Bah! Hoaxers! Paris is filling up with naive Americans. This blasted Exposition. Our countrymen are getting into trouble, needing advice and help. If I had known such falderal would occur, I would have declined my appointment. And you! You were warned. To be taken in by this old charlatan after I alerted you to his reputation and past escapades. A man is judged by the company he keeps, Griswold, and this Le Rennet—"

Considering what I and the old one had been put through, I found the Consul's remarks totally fatuous. "Le Rennet?" I interrupted. "No, sir. You are mistaken. I wish to present the illustrious American Poet, Mister Edgar Allan Poe."

Le Rennet drew himself up and, with a weak smile, bowed. Rathbone's complexion turned florid and he literally huffed in indignation. "Fool. Be damned!" He marched from the room.

Etienne spoke in English, his lips showing the shadow of a smile. "I feel I should apologize for my colleague in rescue." The old man waved him into silence. "It was nothing." The Prefect spoke with the official in rapid French and ended by signing a stamped and seal-laden document. "You may go now. But given the charge against you and its source, I beg you to be careful. Your release could be revoked."

At that moment, Le Rennet collapsed. I had neither the strength nor the quickness to catch him before he sprawled at my feet. With the help of a gendarme, Etienne and I propped the old man in the back of a police carriage and sped home.

The instant of our arrival, Etienne and I ministered to the old man. From a drawer in his room, I obtained additional nitrate pearls and they brought him around in short order. His spirits were of the best. Our clothing was removed and burned by Etienne in our kitchen stove. "I fear you have been keeping bad company," he said, as we heated water to wash and delouse ourselves. "The accommodations are not such as to attract many tourists, heh?"

Despite my sensitivity to the dreadfulness of our incarceration, I found myself buoyed by the Prefect's joviality. After we had bathed—twice!—Etienne prepared a solution to treat our wounds. "Use Bob's Oil," suggested Le Rennet in keeping with the mood. Etienne dispatched the *gendarme*, who returned with bowls of a hearty soup, the best nourishment to start with, according to Etienne, if we wished to avoid severe cramps and nausea. But we did consume bumpers of wine, beautiful red wine, and laughed uproariously as the Prefect detailed the not unserious problems Le Rennet's activities had caused for the officialdom of three countries. As the old man dozed happily before a crackling fire, Etienne made his departure. At the door, I embraced him in the French style, thanking him as best I was able. Then I asked him a question I would have put earlier but for the old man's collapse.

"What day is this?"

"It is Sunday, Monsieur. *Bonsoir. Et bonne chance.*"

I stood upon the steps, glorying in what the poet so aptly described as "a beauteous evening, calm and free." I revelled in freedom, and on a whim, since everything seemed in order, I softly closed the door and set out upon a postprandial stroll.

The crowded, twisting streets were wonderfully vibrant. There was merriment in the air, as if life itself were being toasted. I came to a Roman church, St. Germain des Pres. I am not a religious man. While in Paris I had failed to attend a single service, choosing not to inconvenience myself by going out of my way in search of a Protestant church. But now I entered St. Germain. The interior was dimly lit and cool. In the stillness, there was peace. I was alive. I was free. I was extremely grateful.

When I returned, Le Rennet was still asleep in his chair. The fire was cold ashes, so I threw a coverlet over him and quietly retreated.

"If Prince Rudolph committed suicide," came the old man's voice from behind me, "why was there no weapon found in his room? Good night, Master Griswold. And thank you."

CHAPTER

*A troop of Echoes, whose sweet duty
Was but to sing,
In voices of surpassing beauty
The wit and wisdom of their king.*

ANYONE MADE COGNIZANT OF THE OLD MAN'S RECENT OR-
deal, his age, and his prior physical condition would con-
fidently predict a long period of recuperation and a necessary
curtailment of our involvement in the *affaire* Mayerling. Over
the months, however, I had acquired some knowledge of the
"phrenology" of his mind, or, at least, his spirit. True, after
a fashion, we rested for a week, both plagued particularly by
painful pullings and twitchings caused by the rat bites. Fortunately, there was no infection, and our wounds healed
tolerably, leaving but the barest traces. A thin pink line ran
down the old man's right jaw. A similar, though longer line
emerged from my upper lip onto my right cheek. Three short
marks, two upon my left wrist and hand, one upon my right
thumb, are also visible to this day. Even now I often dream
of rats and awake in a sweat. Moreover, I am inordinately
fearful of the vermin, regardless of size.

During that week of inactivity, Le Rennet remained in

character. He was mulish! He would pull himself from bed and stomp about. When I pleaded with him to sit down, he would curse and wave his stick at me—a walking stick being his only concession to his weakened condition. We had but one visitor, a rough-looking man who delivered a parcel containing my notebook, our German dictionary, and the old man's reading glass. Also a warning from Ida Illyes to avoid the Baron.

"Why haven't we heard from Evans?" Le Rennet demanded as each post arrived. I had no answer. To distract him, I purchased the newspapers for the period of our captivity. We spent hours poring over them, and found but one item of note. The *Gazette des Tribunaux* printed an account of Rudolph's death which it claimed was being suppressed by the authorities in Vienna: Archduke Johann Salvator had killed the Crown Prince! Present at Mayerling on that fatal night, he had made some jest about Mary Vetsera. Rudolph then insulted Salvator, who then slapped Rudolph, who then drew his revolver and fired wildly. Salvator then struck Rudolph with a champagne bottle, smashing his skull. Mary Vetsera had been killed by one of Rudolph's wild shots.

"Nonsense," growled Le Rennet. "They were the closest of friends, and Salvator was in Fiume on the night of Rudolph's death."

"If Evans' report is accurate," I added. I should not have mentioned the dentist, for Le Rennet was off again, demanding to know why we had received no letter or other communication from him. He groused and grumbled through that day and the next, disregarding virtually every effort I made to guard his health. To my great relief, the answer to his question came on Sunday, exactly one week after our release.

I opened the door in answer to a heavy pounding and there stood an indignant Evans. "Where in the devil have you been? I called practically every day last week and got no answer. So I joined Mery for a few days at Madame Lascaut's. The old hippopotamus bored me silly, but Mery seemed to enjoy the guests." He finally took in what was before his very eyes. "My God! What has happened to you both?"

"Rats," I replied, and Le Rennet succinctly described our imprisonment, omitting many of the more horrifying details.

"You are fortunate to be among the living," the dentist said —unnecessarily, I thought.

"You are looking healthy, sir," I commented, having observed that he had added some few pounds during his stay in Vienna.

"The tortes at the Sacher are irresistible," he said, thumping his girth. When he opened his coat, I noted that he was girdled with a red silk sash. "Of course. Very popular. In Vienna, everyone wears one—counts to waiters, everyone. Very stylish!" I personally thought he looked ready for a part in a comic opera.

Le Rennet poured brandy, toasted the dentist, and got immediately to the subject. "What do you have for us?"

"First, Elisabeth has fled Vienna. She said she could not abide the place. Probably she's gone to Corfu. As soon as she left, I was summoned by the Lord Marshal and the household minister. They told me my services were no longer needed, that my leaving Vienna would be most appreciated. In fact, they had already assisted me by cancelling my room at the Sacher. I would find rail passage awaiting me when I called for my luggage. It was all very neatly handled, I must say."

"And Elisabeth? No final message?"

"I was examining her excellent teeth for the last time when she said to tell you that she fears for your spiritual life. She has arranged to send you a priest."

"Excellent, excellent!" Le Rennet sang out, picking up the dentist's word. He fairly bubbled and quickly poured another round of brandy. His cheeks flushed and I feared this sudden intemperance. If little else during the past week, he had at least been abstinent—or nearly so.

"He is to arrive on Wednesday next and will wait upon

you at the House of St. Benedict. But don't you fear further interference or reprisals from Baron Metzengerstein?"

"Unlikely yet. He will wait to discover the effects of our sojourn in prison. Besides, he has lodged his complaint, and we are still subject to prosecution. Etienne cannot protect us for long. We must finish quickly."

I asked Evans if there could be any truth to the story printed in the *Gazette*. "Well, Vienna is amuck with rumors and the Salvator version has the virtue of not perpetuating that ridiculous double suicide story."

"Ridiculous?" I objected.

He removed a small note pad from his interior coat pocket, "Ahem. Statement of January 31, 1889, drawn up by the office of the Lord Marshal of His Imperial Royal Apostolic Majesty. Signed by Doctor Heinrich Slatin, Secretary in the Lord Marshal's Office and by Doctor Franz Auchenthaler, Imperial and Royal Court Physician. I quote: 'The Court Physician Doctor Franz Auchenthaler diagnoses undoubted suicide by means of a firearm. In the left frontal bone is a ragged area of loose skin substance, five centimeters long and three centimeters wide, in the neighborhood of which the hair is singed. This, therefore, is the entry point of the projectile—' "

"Are you talking about the Crown Prince or the Baroness?"

"The Baroness, Griswood." The dentist continued to read from his notes. " 'The path of the bullet runs through the brain, ending two centimeters above the right outer ear, there forming a narrow sharp-edged exit. The bones at the entry and exit points are splintered all around. Otherwise, no injury is observable. The injury is absolutely lethal; death must have been instantaneous.' "

"Well, there you have it," I said. "Suicide, as attested to by the physician. How can one quarrel with his findings?"

Evans flipped a page or two. "From a statement made just two weeks ago by Alexander Baltazzi who identified the body of his niece and, with Count Stockau, removed the body from

Mayerling for burial at Heiligenkreuz. Again, I quote. 'Under the flickering light of a lantern, we were led to the room where the corpse of the poor, beautiful Baroness had been laid the day before. The official broke the seals and opened the door—' "

"Get on with it," urged Le Rennet.

Evans was clearly affronted by yet another interruption but dutifully turned another three pages. "This you should find most interesting. 'The corpse was still in the same state in which it had been found the day before together with that of the Crown Prince—the eyes wide open and protruding in a fixed stare, the mouth half-agape with a congealed stream of blood welling from it and covering part of the body. The arms resting in the lap, slightly bent, the left hand rigidly clutching a handkerchief which could only be freed from the stiff hand by force. When the body was first discovered in the Crown Prince's room it was lying on its back. But it had been carried from there into another room and placed on a bed and—' "

"That will do," said Le Rennet in a whisper. Then he broke into whooping, coughing laughter from which it took several minutes to recover.

"I thought you would enjoy that," said Evans, preening.

"So, Master Griswold?" demanded the old man, rising from his chair and again filling our glasses with brandy. The bottle emptied, he flung it into the fireplace. "Well?" he shouted, turning to face me. I remained silent, not knowing what he expected. He shook his head and muttered in German. Giggling, the dentist translated: " 'Against stupidity even the gods struggle in vain.' "

"The left hand, Griswold." There was a kind of frantic jubilation in the old man's voice. "The left hand! Good God, no wonder the mother was forbidden to visit Mayerling, or even to have her daughter's body brought to Vienna. No wonder Mary Vetsera was buried, literally and figuratively, in a rural cemetery. Death was instantaneous, caused by a bullet entering the left side of her head. Yet when she was discovered, her arms were folded. In her left hand she clutched a handkerchief, clutched it in a death grip. She was murdered."

"All right, sir, all right. She was murdered. By Rudolph, obviously, since he was the only one present. It is shocking to think of the Crown Prince as a murderer. Yet a different kind of suicide pact is still possible. At her request, might not Rudolph have killed her before doing away with himself?"

"I have some information about Rudolph, too, if you want it," said Evans.

"I want more brandy," Le Rennet announced. "I knew murder had been done."

"But how could you know it, if the information was not actually available until a short time ago? Intuition?" I asked mockingly.

"Intuition is but the conviction arising from those inductions or deductions of which the processes are so shadowy as to escape our consciousness, elude our reason or defy our capacity. I knew. I want more brandy!"

"Damn the brandy!" I bellowed in frustration. "You still have not answered my question."

"And I will have more brandy. I am tired of sitting in that damn chair, I am tired of this house. You may join me if you wish," he said to Evans and me. Remorseful over my display of temper and worried for his health, I declined the invitation, as did the dentist. Ignoring our objections, he donned his old tattered cloak, picked up his walking stick and set forth. Despite an assumed nonchalance, he was greatly agitated and we could see that his face was bloodless, that his hand shook nearly causing him to trip over his cane. He was in a concentrated state of intoxication, but fortunately the coolness of the night air had its effect. His mental energy began to yield to its influence, though he continued to talk incoherently, to exhibit confused perceptions. Long before we reached a cafe, he collapsed and between us we carried him back to his bed.

"The old fool," said Evans, with a touch of sympathy in his voice.

"Many things," I said softly, "but not a fool."

"You're right, Griswold. He is a *fantast*. But I've known him for nearly a decade and it's astounding how often his fantasies have proven, in the end, to be gospel truth."

Blessed Monday! By midday I had teeth! The old man awoke before me and I found him at the table, a mug of black coffee in front of him. He looked frazzled and spoke contritely. "I am afraid my recollection of last night is extremely hazy, Griswold, and I imagine that I gave you some trouble."

"Think nothing of it, sir. Are you sure you should be up and about?"

"I will manage. But tell me. I remember Evans' arrival, of course, and then a sense of exhilaration—accompanied by too much brandy, apparently. But the source of that feeling . . ."

"The Baroness. In her left hand—"

"That's it." He gulped his coffee. "We must visit Evans. I need more facts to chew on. And you, I think it is time you got your absent teeth replaced. Do not chide me. I could not possibly rest."

We were warmly welcomed by Evans, who did indeed motion me to his treatment chair. Le Rennet sprawled upon the couch. "Now tell me what you learned of Rudolph," he said.

"Doctor Widerhofer, the Imperial Physician-in-Waiting, went to Mayerling the morning Rudolph's death was reported. He mentioned seeing a pistol beside the bed, but no such weapon was ever discovered, despite a thorough inventory. So that situation remains as I reported it to you."

"And ammunition?"

"The Commission of Inquiry found one bullet lodged in a table. That was a week or more after Rudolph was buried.

It was presented to Franz Joseph. According to Elisabeth, the Emperor had it mounted as a relic.

"How *bizarre*," I managed to say before Evans began molding a wax substance onto my gums.

"Again according to Elisabeth, the only personal grief expressed by the Emperor was on the day that suicide was presented as the cause of his son's death. 'He died like a tailor.' That was his sole comment."

I made a questioning sound.

"Griswold, most civilians are unhappy to be conscripted into His Majesty's Imperial Army. They see no particular honor in dying for the Empire and are always deserting under fire. Professional officers have derided tailors, especially, for cowardice. To die like a tailor, therefore, is to die an ignominious death."

"Does His Majesty actually believe that?" asked Le Rennet. "And what does Elisabeth think now?"

"Franz Joseph seems to have accepted suicide. But the Empress? No, not yet, or not completely. One reason is a nun, a Sister Catherine, who has a reputation for making accurate predictions. They are a product of visions. Ridiculous! Three years ago she was in Vienna in order to collect donations for an orphanage she had established. She arrived in time for the Corpus Christi procession. Franz Joseph and Rudolph were, as usual, participants. In any event, she no sooner saw the Crown Prince than she had a vision. In brief, her vision, as she interpreted it for Franz Joseph and Elisabeth, meant that Rudolph would die a violent death if he continued in his dissolute behavior. After Rudolph's death, the Emperor and Empress invited Sister Catherine back to Vienna; they were distraught parents who wished to be put in touch with their son. Imagine! Well, the nun refused to come, saying that she had another vision of Rudolph. She had seen all and did not wish to be subjected to confusing questions. However, she added, they should not grieve overly since the Prince could earn eternal salvation with the aid of masses said for him.

He had not committed suicide. Well, Le Rennet, Elisabeth will not forget those words. Visions! What twaddle." He removed the wax impression.

"Claims like that of the nun have yet to be scientifically investigated and verified. That is a fact. What others do you have concerning Rudolph?"

The dentist disappeared into a further room and returned holding a document of several pages. He began to read. " 'Following the dissection of the body of His Imperial and Royal Highness, the most serene Crown Prince Rudolph, performed at the Imperial and Royal Hofburg in Vienna on January 31, 1889, in accordance with the statutory rules and by the medical specialists appointed to do so by the law, an expert opinion was issued on the strength of the officially recorded findings of the dissection and vouchsafed by the signature of the physicians concerned. Its full text is as follows: Firstly, His Imperial and Royal—' "

"Enough!" I cried. "My teeth, sir. I have had sufficient Imperial-and-Royal whatever."

"A point well taken, Master Griswold. Might we dispense with official expressions and employ plain English?"

Pouting, Evans dropped the document on a side table. "You have no idea how much trouble I went to in order to obtain this document. Now you are not even interested!"

"On the contrary, I am most interested. How did Rudolph die?"

"As a result of his skull being shattered, as well as the anterior parts of the brain. Said shattering was produced by a shot fired against the right anterior temporal area at the closest range. The bullet exited from a wound above the left ear. Again, death was instantaneous. Officially, there is no doubt that Rudolph fired the shot himself."

We waited, but Le Rennet was lost in thought. "The top of his skull was shattered?" he finally asked.

"Yes."

"And the bullet entered his right temple, exiting above his

left ear having followed, apparently, a straight course? How could the top of his skull be shattered? Impossible."

"The official report suggests that the revolver's being held so close to the temple allowed the escaping powder gases to cause that devastation."

"Interesting. We shall see. Anything else? Rumors? Suspicions?"

"A persistent rumor about broken glass littering the Prince's bed and some particles of glass imbedded in his head. Nothing of the sort was mentioned in the official autopsy."

"Anything else in the autopsy? No other wounds, no—"

"Good God, man! The top of Rudolph's head was nearly blown off, as well as part of his face. They resorted to minor surgical reconstruction with wax and paint just to restore him enough for public viewing. The doctors were under extreme pressure to quickly establish the cause of death."

"You mean they did not perform a complete autopsy? They examined nothing but his head?"

"From everything I could learn, they did not."

"And who were these doctors?" asked Le Rennet, suddenly sitting upright with an air of anticipation. Evans consulted his document. "It seems there were several people milling about the billiard room that night—"

"Billiard room?"

"Yes! The billiard room of the Hofburg. The site of the autopsy. As I repeat, there were representatives from Franz Joseph present. The physicians were sent for. They—"

"Who were these doctors?" Le Rennet asked again.

"That's what I was going to tell you. Stop interrupting! The principal examination and dissection were performed by Doctor Herman Widerhofer, Imperial Physician-in-Waiting; Doctor Hans Kundrath of the Institute of Pathological Anatomy; and Doctor Edouard Hofmann, professor of Forensic Medicine."

"Had all three treated Rudolph before? Were they familiar, intimately familiar, with his maladies?"

"Doctor Widerhofer undoubtedly treated Rudolph. But why?"

Le Rennet recounted Krafft-Ebing's revelations about the health, mental and physical, of the late Crown Prince. "Tragic, but fascinating," Evans said. At last he got back to the work at hand. He scooped bits of bone from a box and began to pare, then file them to size.

"Does it not seem odd that Doctor Krafft-Ebing, an outsider who had never before treated or examined Rudolph, diagnosed his condition with but one meeting, a condition which the court physicians had either misdiagnosed or decided to say nothing of?" There was a silence while Evans concentrated upon his work. Finally he fitted the artificial teeth into my mouth. He lit a spirit lamp, melted some metal strips, and molded them around the two new teeth to hold them temporarily in place. Eventually, thin strands of wire secured the two teeth to their natural brothers on each side.

"What of Kundrath and Hofmann? Would they have treated Rudolph? For anything?"

"Probably not," admitted the dentist, tilting his head to the side and studying his work with admiration. "It's finished," he said, handing me a glass. I stared at myself, smiled broadly. The new teeth were somewhat whiter than my own but otherwise indistinguishable therefrom. "Perfect, sir," I said, and for the first time in weeks, I did not whistle my words!

"Perfect indeed," said Le Rennet. But when I turned to smile at him, he was staring at the floor, abstracted. A moment later, however, he arose. "A definite improvement, Griswold, and a thorough piece of work in Vienna, Thomas. I do, indeed, appreciate the trouble you went to. Might I ask one more favor?"

"No," said Evans. "Absolutely not. All those weeks lost. I must think of my practice. With all the visitors to the Exposition, I hope to recuperate my losses. Which reminds me, Griswold, you owe me ten dollars."

"Dollars? Ten of them?"

"Precisely."

"The favor, Thomas," said Le Rennet, "is that you turn over to us your notes and the autopsy document."

"In that case," replied the dentist, "I'll be happy to oblige. Just a minute. I'll get the notes." While we waited for Evans, I reflected that to have my teeth restored, to once more speak normally was worth almost anything. I determined not to quibble with the dentist over his fee.

"But it's an emergency!" came a cry from the foyer. A fellow American. It appeared that Evans' hopes would be realized.

"Here you are," he said upon his return. He handed me the notes and document, then escorted us to his entranceway. "I will be with you shortly, sir," he told the pacing man who held a flannel cloth to his jaw. "Griswold," I said to the stranger. "Wilmot Rufus Griswold, from the fair state of Maryland." "Errah rah," was the muffled response. "Rest assured, sir, that you will get the best of care," I added heartily. We bade Evans farewell and hurried home.

Etienne was awaiting us, seated comfortably in Le Rennet's favorite chair. "I hope you are not offended," he said, waving at the door with a ring of keys. "You are in good spirits," he observed to Le Rennet, as I poured wine for us all. The Prefect frowned. "Have you renewed your investigation? So soon? Are you sure you have recovered sufficiently to deal with this, this overwhelmingly complex problem? And—"

"But does not the entireness of the complex hint at the perfection of the simple?" the old man asked, wreathed in smiles. More conceits. Even Etienne was frankly puzzled. "Simple?" He raised a quizzical eyebrow. "Are you positive? Have you proof?"

"Not in the physical sense of proof. Not yet. But the Calculus of Probabilities, eh? Tomorrow morning, Etienne, would you care to accompany us on a brief journey? To obtain what you might consider *proof*?"

The Prefect's face assumed a worried expression. "To where, Monsieur? I was just about to remind you of the peril in which you still stand."

"To St. Cyr. Shall we say at eight in the morning?"

"But what do you hope to accomplish at the military academy?"

"We shall shoot at some targets. It should not take long. If you can spare the time . . ." Le Rennet let the statement hang.

"Eight o'clock, then. I will bring a carriage," promised an unhappy Etienne. We ate a meal and then the old man instructed me to include Evans' information in my own notebook. As it turned out, I was saved considerable copying. Since the dentist's note pad was several inches smaller than my *cahier*, and since he wrote only on one side of a page, I was able to paste the sheets into my book. I groaned, however, when I turned to the autopsy document. It was in German! "Well, what did you expect, Master Griswold?" Le Rennet laughed. "But I will help you." So, between the two of us and the dictionary, we translated and entered relevant portions.

The old man was abroad before sunrise, and we broke our fast and dressed in a leisurely fashion, although his excitement was evident. Etienne arrived early and attempted to convince Le Rennet of the futility of his journey. "But suppose they refuse to see you?" he argued.

"Colonel Ronflette, of military intelligence, will see us. I am sure of it. After all, he has found good use for my cipher stick and would be most distressed if I were to make its principles public. Get your notebook, Griswold."

"En route!" shouted Etienne to the driver. Having travelled some dozen miles or so south of the city, we passed the palace at Versailles, which reflected a vanished splendor in the morning light. "The old park of Louis XIV," said Etienne to me, "and there is St. Cyr." The vista was magnificent: an immense

stone structure, with stately garden, sculptured hedges, and parade grounds where uniformed ranks marched smartly. "It hardly looks a military academy," I said.

"It was a convent until the Revolution," explained Le Rennet. "Madame de Maintenon kept an exclusive boarding school there for well-born but perhaps not so well-monied young girls. Jean Racine wrote two of his plays expressly for her students. If you wish we might pay our respects to Madame. Her tomb is preserved in the chapel."

We were announced and almost immediately received. Colonel Ronflette was a balding man of moderate height. A small pair of gold-rimmed spectacles rested across a large nose. Surprisingly, given what must have been his elevated position, his uniform seemed simplicity itself. Le Rennet, whom he greeted enthusiastically, introduced Etienne and me. I was pleased to think that my French, though still unequal to involved conversation, was adequate for the social amenities. At least the Colonel did not wince as we exchanged pleasantries.

Le Rennet having expressed his desire to use the armory, a subaltern was dispatched to prepare for our arrival. We left the main building. The Colonel and the old man strolled ahead of Etienne and me. We crossed a garden and entered an out-building, descending a flight of steps which caused me a twinge of recollection. Will such dark and stony structures always remind me of dungeons? We entered a large hall. Rack upon rack of rifles were neatly arranged along the length of it. We paused before the half-door of a smaller room, where a soldier saluted sharply and retreated upon an order from the Colonel. He returned momentarily, bearing three hand weapons. The Colonel signed for them and led us across the armory to yet another chamber. Inside, wooden brackets held targets of various sizes. Bags and boxes were filled with sand, as were two open pits on the floor.

The Colonel laid the weapons on a table. He spoke to Le Rennet, and Etienne quietly translated for me. "We, too, were interested, of course. The rumors, the reports which seem to prevaricate, the missing links, as you say. These are the weapons which Crown Prince Rudolph was known to have in his possession. A reliable source reports that he frequently slept with these two under his pillow." The Colonel pointed to two of the weapons, then handed one of them, a deadly looking pistol, to Le Rennet.

"Griswold, are you ready? I want you to take down the description of each weapon." While the Colonel spoke, Le Rennet dictated the particulars of the first weapon: "An Austrian Army revolver, Mark 74, Gasser System, eleven millimeter bore, thirty-five centimeters long, a newly modified drum holding six rounds." The Colonel passed the second one to Le Rennet. "An Austrian Infantry Officer's revolver, Mark 74, Gasser-Krobateschek System." The old man spelled the unfamiliar word for me. "Slightly smaller than the first. A nine millimeter bore, and just twenty-three centimeters long. Its drum, too, holds six rounds." Le Rennet offered the weapon to Etienne.

"Most efficient," said the Prefect, "and handsome." He gave it to me. It was indeed well-crafted, certainly much superior to those I had seen long ago during my experience at war. "But how can the Colonel be sure that these were the weapons in Rudolph's possession?"

"In our world," replied Etienne, "allies and enemies change places with astonishing rapidity, not to mention regularity. It is the Colonel's duty, as an intelligence officer, to be sure that France receives no surprises concerning the armaments of potential enemies. The Colonel, I am convinced, does his job with typical French thoroughness."

Le Rennet examined the third weapon, a much smaller pistol, resembling in size the Derringer. "A common Bulldog revolver, seven millimeter bore; again, the drum holds six rounds."

"Bulldog?" I asked.

"An accurate description," said Etienne. "It was developed

for civilian use by people in carriages, by horsemen, by bicyclists—all of whom are often attacked by dogs."

At a nod from Le Rennet, the Colonel loaded the Bulldog from a case of cartridges. He led us to a wooden target flanked by artificial earthen walls. Even though I watched him take aim and fire, I was startled by the noise. He gave the weapon to Le Rennet, who touched the barrel of the Bulldog to the wood of the target before he fired. He repeated this procedure twice. Then, returning the weapon to the Colonel, the old man got down on hands and knees behind the target, arising finally with two of the spent bullets. "They would not carry far at all," he observed. When he translated his remark into French, the Colonel agreed with him.

Le Rennet next inspected the front and back of the inch-thick target. "Griswold," he called. I joined him. "Look. Remember? Slight splintering around the entry and exit points. Like these." He pointed to three scorched, splintered holes in the target. "Mary Vetsera?" I asked. Le Rennet nodded.

The process was repeated with the two remaining weapons, the Colonel shooting from point-blank range into thicker targets. The explosions were deafening. Le Rennet examined each hole. Finally, he asked the Colonel to snub the nose of two bullets, and, again, the two larger weapons were fired at fresh targets. The flattened projectiles tore gaping holes in them. "And what do you think?" Etienne translated the question Le Rennet put to the Colonel. "The bullet entered the right temple and left an exit wound above the left ear, shattering the top of the Crown Prince's skull. Could that have been done by either of these weapons?"

The Colonel merely shrugged. In fact, he said nothing until we were seated in our carriage. Just before he closed the door, he spoke softly with Le Rennet. "The Colonel has heard of our troubles with Metzengerstein, Griswold," Le Rennet said as we left St. Cyr. "He contends that no known weapon could have produced the wound which killed the Crown Prince. He is certain of it. But his opinion was given in strictest confidence."

"The Colonel is an exemplary officer," Etienne said. "He is truly representative of our superior military ability and might."

"No doubt, the Colonel is assiduous," said Le Rennet. "But, unlike Rudolph, he is preparing to fight the last war, not the next. He is not alone. Rudolph observed that, for a time, the Emperor had adjusted to the nineteenth century. The pity of it is, that Franz Joseph should be adjusting to the twentieth."

"Your opinion, sir," I teased. "Does the new century begin on January first, 1900 or 1901?"

"I fear it has already begun," he answered pensively, and my lighthearted mood vanished as suddenly as the sun being swallowed by a cloud.

CHAPTER

> . . . *the intellect suffers to pass*
> *unnoticed those considerations*
> *which are too obtrusively and too*
> *palpably self-evident.*

THE FOLLOWING MORNING, WEDNESDAY IT WAS, FOUND LE Rennet in a state of extreme excitation. In the twilight of a summer day, I have been startled to suddenly find myself in the midst of swarming midges, all engaged in frantic, ceaseless activity. Though I am not fanciful, Le Rennet's condition reminded me of them. It was as if every fiber of his body pulsed, every particle or element wildly vibrated. I was alarmed. Might not the frail bonds which held him together break?

Before the tenth hour had chimed, he was into the wine. When he finished it, he told me to fetch a bottle of brandy. "Sir, I am hardly a Prohibitionist, as you surely know. But still, some moderation—"

"I do not drink for stimulation," he stated in a controlled voice. "I drink for rest. Moreover, there are few men of extraordinary profundity who are found wanting in an inclination for the bottle." Rather than intensify his nervous state with argument, I did as he ordered, purchasing both brandy and wine. By the time we ate our noon meal of cheese and bread, accompanied by the wine, I noted that his agitation had indeed eased.

Soon after, Le Rennet brushed his old coat in preparation for our visit to Father Degrote. "I miss that suit," he said sadly. "It had to be burned, of course, but I was quite fond of it. Did you know, Griswold, that in the last dozen or so years I spent in the United States as Edgar Allan Poe, I never once owned a fine suit of clothes? Never."

"Like Rudolph, sir," I said, going along with his mood. "As he was a prophet so you were a genius without honor in your own land."

"You might say so, Griswold. You might indeed say so. Like Rudolph."

It was market day in our quarter of the city, and we had to walk among the colorful throng for some distance before we secured a hack. Carefully, the driver picked his way amid the pedestrians and carts which lined the streets, then crossed the Seine and soon deposited us before the high iron fence which bore the name and crest of a Benedictine order. We were welcomed courteously by a young seminarian and led into a cool, modestly appointed room whose only source of light was two high, narrow windows. The silence could be felt—a comforting silence, airy and calm.

"Don Gregorio Degrote," said the priest who joined us.

"Henri Le Rennet, Father. And here is my associate, Mr. Wilmot Griswold. I believe you were expecting us."

"I was told you would visit, sir, and that I might have an opportunity to practice my English." A smile momentarily played about his lips. "But I was not informed of the nature of your business. How may I help you?"

"It is about your recent voyage, Father," began Le Rennet, and the priest smiled ruefully, shaking his head. "I feared as much," he said, throwing his eyes heavenward. "It has become a burden, that tale." He paced to the opposite side of the room, thoughtfully, as though making up his mind. He was taller than I, but extremely thin so that the neck above his cassock seemed an unsteady stalk. I noted that his surcingle was wound twice about his waist and yet hung nearly to his knees. As he passed the windows, his features were plainly visible. His thick brown hair was combed forward over his temple. Large brown eyes dominated his face. His skin was dark and leathery.

"So you wish to know about this mysterious Vicomte de Montreine." He stood before us, a challenge in his posture.

"If you would be so kind, Father," said Le Rennet.

"Very well," he answered peremptorily. "In 1878, I was sent to Dacca, as a missionary. I remained there until last January when I was recalled. I sailed from Bombay, and arriving at Aden, I changed ships, boarding the British steamer *Parramatta*. At Port Said, we took several passengers aboard."

"On what day was that, Father?" asked Le Rennet.

The priest responded as though reciting a litany or telling his familiar beads. "The ship was bound for London, with stops at Port Said, Brindisi, Malta, Gibraltar, and Plymouth. We left Port Said around noon, on Wednesday, the twenty-ninth of January. We arrived at Brindisi on Friday, the first day of February, also around midday. Shortly thereafter, in Rome, I informed my superior of the odd encounter with this Vicomte de Montreine. I had no idea that the story . . ." he paused, smiled gently, "that the story would cause such notoriety for a simple priest."

"You were unaware of the death of the Crown Prince until you docked at Brindisi?" I asked.

"I knew nothing of the catastrophe until I left the ship. Of course, the city was talking of little else, so my ignorance was soon dispelled."

"But Vicomte de Montreine?" asked Le Rennet. "I believe you reported that he informed you of Rudolph's suicide on the morning of January thirtieth, while you were still at sea, distant from all land."

"He did, but I certainly did not believe him. The Vicomte, as I recall, was travelling with a party on the first-class deck. I had passage in second class. I was standing at the side rail, looking at the rolling sea, trying to calm my stomach. He simply approached and introduced himself. He chatted briefly, then asked if I had heard the news. 'What news?' I asked. 'Why, that His Highness, Crown Prince Rudolph, has taken his own life.' I told him that I had heard no such thing and fervently prayed that the world would be spared such a tragedy. I recall I also made some slight remark about humor in poor taste."

"What language did he speak?" asked Le Rennet.

"French. Fluently. With a faint accent. But not a Belgian one. I myself am from Belgium and, naturally, have no difficulty recognizing the dialects of my countrymen."

"What happened next?" I asked eagerly.

"Next he smiled, mockingly I thought, and apologized. He left me standing at the rail, and I did not see him again until we left the ship at Brindisi. He mentioned something about booking rail passage to Brussels, so I replied casually, indifferently, saying that my order was based in the Brabant."

"Could you describe this man, Father?" asked Le Rennet.

Again, the priest rolled his eyes heavenward, his pupils disappearing beneath his lids. Wearily, he sat in a tufted chair, crossed his hands, and fell back, relaxing for what he seemed to regard as a most distasteful undertaking.

"He was average in height, or perhaps slightly above average. He wore a hat and muffler against the weather, so I could see nothing of his hair. He seemed to be in his middle years. I recall he was clean-shaven. That is all. Oh yes, his eyes were irritated by the salty spray."

"Nothing else?" Le Rennet asked with some urgency.

For a moment, the rueful smile returned to the priest's lips.

"Monsieur, I had been upon the sea for many, many days. Our Lord, in his infinite mercy, granted me a safe voyage. But in his infinite wisdom, Our Lord did not choose to lay his hand upon the waters to calm them. I suffered from *mal de mer* for the entire voyage. I fear I did not welcome this Vicomte, nor pay him and his story much heed. I was grateful when he left me alone in my suffering. I am a fisher of men, not a fisherman." Again, a smile flickered. He arose. "I can tell you nothing more. Now, if you will excuse me, I have duties to perform."

Le Rennet was polite, but I discerned disappointment in his farewell to Father Degrote. As I took my own leave, I commented upon his fine grasp of our language. "Yes, English is a useful language. My next mission, in fact, will be to your country, Mr. Griswold. My order is sending me to attend the spiritual needs of the red Indians in America. To a place called Oklahoma, to work among the tribe called the Cherokees."

"Of course! We had forgotten," Le Rennet said boisterously. "Mr. Griswold was delighted when he heard you would be sent to America. Just recently he took up a subscription from his countrymen who are attending the Exhibition here, a small gift to assist your worthy efforts. As you know, there is much to be done amongst our red brethren."

"That was exceedingly kind of you, sir," he said to me, as I attempted not to look foolish.

Le Rennet continued: "Unfortunately, we neglected to stop at our bank to withdraw the funds. If we leave immediately, there is still time before closing. With your permission, Father Degrote, we shall return this evening with our slight contribution."

"But that is unnecessary. You could—"

"But we insist. It would be no trouble. And it would in some small way repay you for your help this afternoon. Shall we say at eight?"

"If you wish," the priest said, without enthusiasm.

The old man stood in the gutter chuckling as he waved his stick to attract a passing cab. Inside, he squeezed my arm affectionately. "Brilliant, Master Griswold. That was inspired." He grinned and chuckled again. I just shook my head; something told me that I did not wish to know why he had lied so outrageously, and to a priest!

To my surprise, our journey home included a stop at the Prefecture of Police. Briskly, without his cane, the old man alighted and disappeared into the building, another one of those large, stone, gloomy affairs. After some moments, during which I distracted myself by admiring the uniforms of the *gendarmes* and the bevy of attractive young women who surrounded them, he returned, a slim box in one hand and an anxious Alexandre Etienne holding the other, earnestly talking. The Prefect nodded to me and, as Le Rennet entered, said grimly, "Be careful. Please, be careful."

The old man dropped to the seat. Off and on humming cheerfully to himself, he stared out the window. My reaction was of an opposite nature, and in the extreme. Whether his manner itself, Etienne's warning, or the ugly memory reawakened by that building was the immediate cause of the panic that welled up within me, I do not know. "What more do you plan?" I demanded. "What new misadventure will you lead us into, from which, unlike the renowned knight of La Mancha, we may not emerge unscathed. Or even alive! What madness holds you now?" In truth, I even wished I had never met Mery Laurent or made that puerile wager.

At length he replied in a soft voice, looking directly into my eyes. "Not madness, Griswold, but reason, although there are moments when, even to the sober eye of reason, the world of our sad humanity may assume the semblance of Hell. We must go forward now. We have no choice left us. Or at least, I do not." He gazed straight ahead into the blank wall of our carriage. I said nothing. I am not even sure that I thought. But when we arrived at our lodgings, I followed him, carrying his case. It was of moderate size, quite light, but heavily clasped. In stark red letters on its front was written: SAC DE PHYSIOGNOMIQUE, which conveyed nothing to me.

Immediately he began issuing orders, as was his wont, like a general preparing for battle. "You must hurry, Griswold. Buy a sketch pad and a few charcoal sticks. I will barely have time to teach you." "Teach me what?" I inquired, but he simply waved me to the door with an additional admonition to hurry. I was disgruntled, therefore, when I had to wend my way through several streets before I found a shop with the required supplies—strange indeed in a city famed for its artists.

I returned famished. The Grand Canyon was as nothing compared with the hollow in my abdomen. I suggested I prepare a gumbo. Le Rennet again complained of the lack of time, so we had one more meal of wine, bread and cheese. He seemed satisfied, but I felt that my hunger had only increased.

At once, he opened the case he had obtained from Etienne. Countless shapes cut from colored isinglass spilled onto the table. Upon examination, they proved to be an endless variety of noses, lips, ears, beards, moustaches, and so on—the gamut of human facial features. "It is a concoction of mine to assist Etienne in identifying criminals. By skillfully arranging these bits and pieces, one can form a surprisingly accurate likeness of a human face. It is then but a small matter to trace these pieces in charcoal. The end result is a full facial portrait. The technique can be most useful."

He began by demanding, of all things, that I reconstruct his own facial features! After much hesitation and several false starts, I finally got the most appropriate nose, eyes, eyebrows and other features. As he predicted, the result was accurate, if crude. The next step was more difficult. "My hands have lost their touch for such work," he said, "as have my eyes their sharpness. I must rely upon you, Griswold. When the pieces are in place, you must trace them. Then, with *chiaroscuro*, you must give the outline human life."

Crumpled sheets from the pad littered the table and floor before I achieved a tolerable likeness of the old man's face. In all modesty, I believe it would have been recognized by any of his acquaintances.

"But of what use is this?" I asked. "We have no criminal to identify, unless you are thinking of the elusive Vicomte de Montreine. Even with this aid, Father Degrote will be of little assistance."

"As he is now, you are correct, Griswold. But we may be able to change him subtly so that his faculties of memory are increased. Did you observe that when the good priest lifted his eyes heavenward, his pupils nearly disappeared beneath his lids? Do you recall that when he sat down to relax, his left hand was atop his right in such a position that his left thumb clasped the other, even though he was clearly right-handed?"

"Your point, sir."

"That Father Degrote is of a type most favorable for induction into a mesmeric trance."

I stared at him in disbelief. "You intend to mesmerize the priest? To make a sleep waker of him against his will? Surely, he will not co-operate in such a mad scheme."

"I fear it is the only way, Griswold. We are close to the truth now and Degrote holds the key to unlock it. We must have that key. Our time is running out. No harm shall come to him, I assure you."

"But even supposing for a moment that you are successful at inducing such a trance," I asked weakly, "how will turning the priest into a sleep waker serve that end?" I was the one who poured the brandy now. I had no faith in Le Rennet's ability to use this exotic method. Worse, to so tamper with a person without his permission—especially a priest!—struck me as an invitation to the devil.

"A person so impressed into a trance employs only with effort, and then feebly, the *external* organs of sense. Yet he perceives, with keenly refined perception and through channels supposed unknown, matters beyond the scope of those same physical organs. His intellectual faculties are wonderfully exalted and invigorated. An abnormal condition, I agree, but not sleep, Griswold. It is a condition of profoundest concentration. And within that state of heightened faculties and concentration, the priest will delve downward, much farther downward than he thinks possible, into his memory. Although if you asked him he would disclaim the ability, he will present in detail his mental image of our Count de Montreine. The rest shall depend on you."

I did not doubt the existence or the value of the mesmeric process itself. After all, I had witnessed examples of it upon the better quality lyceum stages and had heard unchallenged reports of near-miraculous cures effected by doctors employing the technique. But, still, the old man's trying it on a priest frightened me. Too far along the road with him to part company, I fortified myself with another brandy and yet another.

"Griswold," said Le Rennet in our cab, "I am not mad, nor am I without experience at inducing trances. In fact, I have often written upon the subject. There are mysteries of the human mind which we have not fathomed, despite such wonders as Eiffel's tower, the steam engine, the telegraphic union of the world. And never are these mysteries exposed to the weak human eye . . . unclosed."

"Are you quoting, sir?"

"Yes. Myself."

All very well, I thought, but I still found the undertaking insane.

This time we were received by Degrote himself, who led us into the same room we had occupied that afternoon, now lit by several lamps. Following Le Rennet's directions, I handed him an envelope of small franc notes and explained the hopes of non-existent subscribers for his success in converting the Indians of Oklahoma from their heathenish ways. I mumbled an answer to his question about my own experience upon the frontier. "Yes, generally speaking, sir, I found the Cherokee extremely placid—except when some act enraged them."

Le Rennet interrupted at this juncture, withdrawing from his pocket a brilliant stone which depended from a silver chain. "This was given to my friend by a Cherokee," the old man lied. "It is said to have curative powers for those people. Their belief, no doubt, rests on the fact that when gazed at intently, the stone appears to change color. From white, to blue, to crimson. . . . Do you see the colors, Father Degrote? How lovely they are, and so many . . . one, two, three, four, five, six . . ."

He continued to count, letting the stone dangle before the fixed stare of the priest. Gradually he moved the chain back. The priest's eyes followed the stone until the moment when Le Rennet slowly passed his hand before them. The trance was evidently consummated, for now the priest stared at the old man. Quickly, Le Rennet exchanged lateral passes for downward ones and directed his gaze entirely into the priest's right eye.

The signs of the mesmeric influence were unequivocal: the glassy roll of the eye gave way to that expression of inward examination which is peculiar to sleep waking. With another few lateral passes, Le Rennet set the priest's eyelids to quivering as if in incipient sleep. One vertical pass closed the eyes altogether. The priest's breathing became so easy, so shallow in fact, that it seemed to stop. Still, the general appearance was certainly not of death, but of utter relaxation.

"Are you asleep?" asked the old man quietly.

"Yes—no! I would rather sleep more soundly."

Le Rennet moved closer to the priest, speaking words I could not hear, touching the priest's forehead with his hands, caressing it, "Do you sleep now?"

"Yes."

"And you will help me, will you not?"

"I shall."

"Do you remember the voyage from Port Said? You were standing by the rail. The sea was choppy, you were feeling most unwell."

"Most unwell," echoed the priest. His voice seemed to reach me from a vast distance, from the bowels of the earth. I was chilled by the sound and so did not at first perceive Le Rennet's frantic waving, the signal for me to silently prepare the *sac* and sketch pad.

"And then a man came up to the railing and talked to you. Do you remember his name?"

"He said he was the Vicomte de Montreine."

"You are absolutely certain that is the name he gave you?"

"Absolutely."

"You will open your eyes and look at me. You will see nothing but what I tell you to see. Do you understand?"

"I understand." His eyes rolled open. He gazed uncomprehendingly at the pad which Le Rennet placed in his lap. We stationed ourselves on either side of him. With skill and patience, Le Rennet placed isinglass features upon the blank pad. "Montreine—did he possess a nose like this? Or like this?"

"No, not like that. No. It was longer, sharper." Hastily I searched our collection of noses and supplied two additional specimens. "Yes, like that. The first one." And so we proceeded through ears, eyes, lips, chins. All the while I feared we would be interrupted, with what danger to the entranced priest I knew not. After an age of sorting and shuffling, the priest acknowledged that the isinglass features which lay upon the pad were a fair representation of the mysterious Vicomte.

"Quickly," hissed Le Rennet. As he spoke soothingly to the priest, I traced the visage, feature by feature; finally I added shading to hollow the cheeks as he described them, and drew a line across the forehead to indicate a hat. Le Rennet took the sketch and placed it upon the priest's lap.

"You will look very closely, please. Is that Vicomte de Montreine?"

The priest studied the sketch. I moved to the door in the hope of intercepting any intruder. "Yes, that is the man," he said at length. Thank God, it was over. Le Rennet again closed the priest's eyes with a pass of his hand. "You will remember nothing, except that you fell asleep while we were talking of Oklahoma. Now!"

The eyes rolled slowly open, the pupils disappearing downward, then upward to meet our gaze. Father Degrote yawned and stretched his arms. "I apologize, gentlemen. I must have dozed. Please forgive me. I found your comments upon American Indians most enlightening, but obviously I am in need of rest." The rueful smile appeared for a moment.

Le Rennet spoke as I hurriedly packed his *sac*, then stood by the doorway. "But of course, Father. It was our fault entirely. My friend is so enthusiastic about Indians that he would keep us listening through the night. Good evening, Father."

"Good evening, and again my thanks for your efforts, Mr. Griswold. Tomorrow morning, I will offer my mass for the benefit of you and your countrymen."

A mass! As we adjourned to a nearby cafe, I silently petitioned the Lord to forgive us our trespasses. My unease was not the least abated by the despondency which now gripped Le Rennet. I said, "Well, is this drawing not a clew? Have we failed? To me, the face is slightly familiar, but then I suppose almost any face would be. I mean, I mean, it does not seem distinctive."

"I realize that, Griswold. Please, let me think." Moodily he sipped his brandy and called for another. Finally, he came to some sort of conclusion, for he placed two notes on the table and left, carrying the sketch pad. I followed with the *sac*, hoping against hope that whatever his decision, it would take us home. But when he hailed a two-wheeler and gave the driver directions, my hope was dashed in a way I could not have imagined.

"No, sir!" Le Rennet in the carriage, I stood firmly upon

the ground and ordered the cabbie to wait. "Absolutely not! The Baron? The very person who so nearly worked our ruin? I shall never dare to enter beneath his roof again. Madness, Le Rennet. It is madness!" Desperately, I looked about me for anyone, any means which would help me dissuade the old man. A *gendarme*? But no. Even though we were in Paris, in Etienne's domain, I could not risk being jailed again. The American Consulate? But even if I could persuade the driver to take us there, Rathbone would have us ejected; even worse, he might make certain that we were once more incarcerated.

"Monsieur," said the driver. "We go. Now." He jiggled the reins, clicked his tongue. The carriage began to move. At the last moment, I flung myself inside.

I paid the driver handsomely and promised more if he would only wait upon our return. "It will not be long, I assure you," I told him. When we arrived, the house was aglitter with lights, and carriages lined the lane. Liveried servants lounged beside them, making remarks as we passed. I certainly was much more aware than they that the old man and I did not belong at the festivities. At the door, the same servant we had occasion to remember greeted us with a snarl and slammed the door in our faces. Le Rennet again pounded, this time with his stick. There was no response, for which I was grateful.

We retreated down the steps and I moved in the direction of the waiting cab. "No," said Le Rennet, pulling at my arm. "We must try the rear entrance." But we were spared creeping around that infamous mansion when the Baroness called to us from the doorway. The gas jets which graced the entrance played upon the wry smile with which she greeted us. "You are, without a doubt, crazy. But do come in." She led us into a cloakroom, filled with hats and furs, which seemed popular despite the warm weather.

"You have teeth!" she laughed in delight as I tried to thank her for her part in our release from the dungeon.

"And you are wearing a dress," I countered, momentarily distracted by her rather revealing ice-blue gown.

"But of course. It is a costume ball. Whatever else should I wear? But why are you here?"

Hurriedly, Le Rennet explained our visit to Father Degrote and the sketch we had obtained. He insisted that as she valued our lives and perhaps her own as well, she would tell no one of what we had found.

"But what have you found?" she demanded impatiently.

"What I had expected." Le Rennet held the sketch pad open before her. While she studied it, I noticed her nose wrinkle, her brows rise, her lips twist slightly. She placed an unlit cigar in her mouth and chewed upon it meditatively, but apparently, like myself, she could make nothing of the sketch. Irritated, Le Rennet whipped a charcoal stick from my pocket and attacked the sketch. With crude strokes he drew in lines representing hair brushed flat. Then with a flourish, more grandiose than artistic, he rubbed the charcoal across the face so that a poor imitation of a hussar's moustache appeared on the face.

Ida Illyes sucked in her breath, uttered a word in what I took to be Hungarian. I felt every fiber of my frame thrill as if I had touched the wire of a galvanic battery. I was staring at the unmistakable visage of Rudolph, the Crown Prince of Austria.

"I am deeply sorry if I have given you a shock, Baroness. But I had to have the spontaneous response of someone who knew Rudolph intimately."

For once the Baroness lost all animation. Indeed, she appeared herself to have slipped into a trance. "Rudolph? Alive? Alive." Her voice as she stared at Le Rennet was almost a monotone.

"Who is alive, my dear?" asked the Baron, entering the cloakroom. "Oh, I see. Our two friends."

"No, Frederick. Not them. *Rudolph.* They claim Rudolph

is alive," she blurted before either the old man or I could stop her. The Baron's puffy face froze. From contemptuous amusement he turned to heated fury. He bellowed for a servant. His hand grasped a candlestick as a cudgel. Disregarding the lighted candle, which fell to the floor, he came toward us, candlestick raised. "Get out. Damn you! Out!" he thundered.

We eased out the door and passed the servants, who were hurrying to the cloakroom. We achieved the cab which, miraculously, stood waiting for us. The driver cracked his whip and we sped off, the noise of a commotion pursuing us as we turned off the lane.

We were safe, and suddenly the face upon the sketch pad loomed before my mind's eye. Yet, for a wild moment or two, my shuddering reason refused to comprehend what I saw. Stupidly, I repeated the words of Ida Illyes, "Rudolph? Alive?"

"I fear, Master Griswold," came the bantering voice of Le Rennet, "that you have lost your wager with Mery Laurent. Like that woman on the urn Mr. Keats describes, she shall forever elude your grasp."

CHAPTER

10

Oh, outcast of all outcasts most
abandoned!—to the earth art thou
not for ever dead?

AND THEN HE DROWSED. IN FACT, BY THE TIME WE REACHED
home, I had to shake him from a surprisingly deep slumber.
I was agog with curiosity. He simply flopped into his favorite
chair, pulled a shawl about his shoulders and closed his eyes.
He seemed drained of all energy except the minimum required
to keep his body functioning. I poured two tots of brandy and
began, "But if that is Rudolph, if the person Father Degrote
saw upon the *Parramatta* was actually the Crown Prince, then
. . . then, what happened at Mayerling?"

His only answer was an inexcusable snore, as if my question
merited no consideration! I sipped the brandy and determined
to begin again. "If that face is the visage of Rudolph," I said,
raising my voice, lacking the patience to be kind.

"*If*, Griswold? But certainly it is. The Prince's situation
had become intolerable. He resolved to act. He had but two
alternatives. He could destroy those around him and seize
power, or he could, so to speak, abdicate. That the former
course would succeed was unlikely. On the other hand, in

choosing the latter course, he could free himself from his official position, and unobserved, unhampered, he might go about his vocation. I recognized his dilemma, having had a similar experience. I saw that he would be driven to *simplicity*, if not deliberately induced to it as a matter of choice. In short, he had to stage his own death in order to be free to act."

"But what occurred, then, at Mayerling? What of Mary Vetsera and Rudolph, or whoever was there that night?" For answer, he resumed snoring. I passed the remainder of the night either prowling about that gloomy manse or fitfully napping in a chair. And, I must confess, in consuming more than an ordinary amount of brandy. Except for his infernal snoring, Le Rennet appeared nearly angelic in his peaceful repose. His features were utterly relaxed so that one might have thought he had mesmerized *himself*.

I was in somewhat of a stupor when a hammering upon our door jolted me out of a dream wherein I stood at the railing of a ship, irresistibly attracted to the waves below me. Disoriented, I took a moment to recall myself. The pounding grew more insistent. Carefully, for I knew not what to expect, I opened the door a crack. It was Etienne, who politely but firmly pushed me aside and closed the door behind him. He walked quickly to the old man and shook him, gently at first, then with vigor.

"Now what has happened?" I asked wearily, my hair tumbling about my eyes and my mouth furry. "What time is it?" asked Le Rennet, surprised to see the Prefect, but rested and alert.

"It is nearly four in the morning," said Etienne.

"You are about early," Le Rennet observed cautiously.

"I have not yet slept. There was a robbery last night, at the Carillon. An American woman had her jewels taken."

"One of those burglars I have heard about?" I asked, "the ones who swing down from the roof on ropes?"

"No, Monsieur. It was her husband. He had taken the jewels to give to his mistress. It is a delicate problem. They are foreigners. Lawfully, the jewels do belong to the man, yet his wife insists that a crime has been committed. She wants him arrested and imprisoned. But enough of *my* problems." His stress on that word kindled foreboding.

"Yes?" Le Rennet prompted.

"I shall go home. I shall retire for a few hours. When I return to my office, there will be an order awaiting me on my desk. I have learned that your stay of prosecution has been revoked. The Baron has long arms, even at one o'clock in the morning. I shall delay, pointing to more pressing criminal matters. But I will not be able to ignore the order for long. By noon at the latest, I must issue the command for your arrest."

"Master Griswold also?" asked Le Rennet.

"Both," Etienne said with finality.

"I believe we will take a trip to the country," the old man said slowly. "If we are not at home when you and your men arrive . . ."

"Naturally, we would be forced to search. But if you are not present, we can do nothing. Of course, this house would be watched."

"Perhaps we could visit—"

"I do not wish to know more, Monsieur. My position is already extremely difficult. Good night." Tall and dignified, the Prefect paused at the door to salute us before he left.

Disconsolate, indeed totally dispirited, I felt incapable of any action. But resilient as ever, Le Rennet quickly swallowed the brandy in his glass and began to move purposefully about the room. "We must pack, Griswold. We must not forget anything of import, for I fear it will be some while before we can return." Having stacked papers and documents, he stopped to survey the room. There was a sadness in his eyes, the kind reserved for taking leave of a dear friend. He retired to his chamber.

I followed his example, and by dawn my trunk and cases stood ready at the door. "It won't do, Griswold. We must travel with minimal baggage since we may have to move about frequently and at short notice." I objected strenuously when he suggested that my sample cases be left behind. "They are far too clumsy, and I doubt if you will transact much business where we are going."

"And where is that?"

"A place where we may practice piscation. Isaak Walton wrote most disarmingly of that art's ability to provide surcease from worries and ample time for meditation."

We ate little, contenting ourselves with bread and coffee as well as a final portion of his tomato concoction. "We must not leave a single scrap of paper behind," he said again as we prepared to depart. "I have it all," I assured him, shouldering my trunk. He pulled the door to and we merged into the morning crowds. We took a few turns and negotiated three intersections before he hallooed a passing hack. His instructions surprised me. "College Rollin? A school?"

"Stephane will help us," he said calmly.

When we arrived, he dismissed the hack and we entered a dank old building which smelled of sweat, urine, chalk dust, and an unidentifiable musty odor. The old man knew his way, nodding in recognition to the occasional official. No one stopped us. We reached a rear room, entered, and stood by the door. A glum M. Mallarme was seated behind a battered desk, his youthful charges buzzing in muted excitement. Laughter and jeers greeted us. Mallarme seemed to drag himself in our direction. The change from the *Mardista* gathering was profound. No longer the sparkling, assured lecturer, he most resembled an old, overworked retainer.

"We must disappear," said Le Rennet without preamble. "Your summer cottage, at Valvins—would it be possible?"

It took Mallarme a moment to digest Le Rennet's words. "Disappear? But why?"

"It is necessary. To know more might place you in jeopardy."

The teacher nodded absently, then turned and shouted at

his class. Several students had raised their slates, on which the word *L'AZUR* appeared. In response, their classmates had started to chant the term. Mallarme stepped into the hall and closed the door, his shout having little effect on the near riot. "Yes. The cottage. A key is kept by Madame Homais. She lives in the village above the apothecary. I will give you a note." He opened the door. The din subsided only fractionally as he rummaged in his desk for pen and paper. Hastily, he wrote our introduction to Madame Homais.

"Good luck, my friend," he said to Le Rennet. "You should not be disturbed. Even in the summer, it is a quiet, sleepy little place. Write, if you are able." They embraced. "And you, Mr. Griswold. You have retrieved your teeth. Good. But have you completed your Epic of Commerce?" The sparkle returned for a moment to his eyes.

"I regret that I have not had the opportunity."

"Ah, but you must let nothing interfere with your poetry. Nothing!" He gripped my hand tightly and again shut himself in with his frolicking students. As we hoisted our baggage, I repeated Mallarme's admonition, with a touch of scorn in my voice. "Nothing? Obviously, he has never been in a dungeon with troops of rats."

"There are worse things, Master Griswold." He did not elaborate but waved down a passing hack. After a ride of a half-hour or so, we stopped at the end of a street which led directly to the banks of the Seine. As we trudged along, the old man exchanged quips with bargemen who lounged against the wharves. At length, he stopped before a dilapidated tub which looked as if it would sink once freed from its moorings. "Pierre?" he called out. A sharp-faced man, grizzled gray hairs upon his chin, emerged and waved. After a short conversation, I was invited aboard, and we cast off.

The journey could have been peaceful, but for the marked contrast between the rhythmic motion of the boat and my internal disquiet caused by consideration of our future. Le Rennet was unperturbed. He spent most of the day talking with Pierre, and later, as I took a brief turn at guiding the barge, they played cards. When I expressed surprise at Pierre's winnings, the old man quietly explained that it was the only way Pierre could be made to accept payment. Toward dusk, we pulled ashore and purchased bread and cheese. Pierre uncorked a great jug of sour red wine, and we made a meal aboard.

When we were again under way, I stood beside Le Rennet, enthralled by the sunset as it painted the fields on either side of the river. I composed lines upon the subject and offered them to Le Rennet: "The soft-sloping meadows lay brightly unrolled, with their mantle of verdure and blossoms of gold."

"Griswold, you are indeed a wonder. Until this moment I cannot recall ever disagreeing with Stephane," Le Rennet remarked, most uncharitably. Lanterns were lit. In silence, the old man studied the river, but the shadowy waters interested me not at all. I was once again determined to understand the revelations of our last night in Paris.

"Do you still maintain that the Crown Prince is alive? That another man died at Mayerling in his place?" I spoke suddenly and apparently startled the old man.

"Murdered, Griswold, murdered. With a cunning and forethought befitting one of the most brilliant minds yet produced by the royal families of Europe. Such a waste!"

"But what you are proposing is preposterous. Rudolph was known to scores, hundreds, perhaps thousands. Someone, surely, would have discovered the hoax."

"Your objection is answered with an ease which is nearly in the ratio of its apparent unanswerability." Obviously the river air suited his conceit-making powers. "Do you recall our first night at the Baron's?"

"Perfectly! I am unlikely ever to forget it."

"We walked for a while before we took a carriage. You specifically observed a *gendarme*. Can you describe him?"

"Of course. He was wearing—"

"Not his uniform, but the man himself!" snapped Le Rennet. Despite great effort, I had to admit that I could recall nothing but the most general characteristics of the man—approximate weight and height. Truly, my attention had been fixed on his dress.

"Precisely. A uniform, in the proper circumstances, is the best of disguises. The gaudier and more ornate, the more successful it will be. Griswold, have you ever seen a photograph or drawing of Rudolph when he was not wearing a uniform?"

In my mind, I reviewed the likenesses of the Crown Prince which had been supplied by the Empress as well as those which had appeared in the Paris newspapers. In all of them, Rudolph wore some manner of uniform. "But the Crown Prince was a stranger to me, like that *gendarme*," I protested. "I must insist that if another had died in his stead, anyone even remotely familiar with Rudolph would have detected the change."

"Not if the impostor had *lived* as the Crown Prince on various occasions over the past five years."

"Would you maintain that his wife, the Princess Stephanie could have been deceived? Ridiculous."

"From a distance, or for short periods of time, she most probably was fooled. You are not thinking, Griswold. He had been estranged from his wife for years, not sharing a matrimonial bed with her. They hardly met, except for formal occasions. Yes, it would be the sort of challenge Rudolph could not resist."

I pondered that for a moment and added triumphantly, "And you will offer a similar explanation for his mother. She could hardly be deceived by a substitute, but then she was hardly ever in Vienna."

"Better, Griswold, better. 'Why are you never here?' wrote Rudolph. Naturally when the Empress did return to the Hofburg for one of her infrequent visits, it was the real Rudolph whom she would see. And Franz Joseph? Ironic, but he unwittingly abetted his son's scheme by dispatching the Crown

Prince on endless missions, missions away from Vienna to the remote edges of the Empire where few could detect in Rudolph's splendid uniform the false from the real Crown Prince. If there should have been some mishap, you must remember with what inordinate skill the Crown Prince cultivated a reputation for erratic behavior. At home, Rudolph was seldom invited into the company of his august father. For many years, Rudolph chafed at that, yet, when he made his decision, the very distance which his father kept between them worked in his favor."

I had listened impatiently, my thoughts racing ahead, for I believed I had discovered the flaw in Le Rennet's reasoning. "But what of the unfortunate Mary Vetsera? She had a most intimate relationship with the Crown Prince. She of all people could not have been deceived by an impostor."

"Have I said she was?" he answered tartly. "On the contrary, she actively aided Rudolph in the deception. That was a stroke of genius on his part. Cruel, but brilliant. The girl added such a magnificent touch of *vraisemblance*! She had to be included, and sacrificed."

I was completely confused. "You mean that the impostor killed her, then himself? Willingly sacrificing his own life in the furtherance of Rudolph's scheme?"

"Surely you must realize by now that they were both killed by Loschek, the Crown Prince's personal servant."

"But why?" I demanded, reaching for a cup of that sour wine. Oddly, Le Rennet refused to join me.

"Why? That is obvious. But that is not the problem." He began a lengthy digression about his early childhood. The major point was this: "When I studied Greek as a youth, I was delighted by Homer. I fell upon his tales of the Olympians with special relish. To be able to give and take away mortal life—as I was growing into manhood, how I longed for that power. Foolishly. Now I have it. I can restore Rudolph to his mother, but then I must immediately take him away from her again, forever. Do I dare to do this? Have I that right?

There, Master Griswold, is the problem." He left me and fell into animated conversation with Pierre.

I drank wine and dozed until awakened by Le Rennet. In darkness, we stumbled the final mile into Valvins. All the while, I cursed our baggage. The old man roused Madame Homais and, after much grumbling and many a suspicious glance, she produced a key. Mallarme's cottage was a simple peasant affair with four small rooms. I observed little else in the weak light of a single candle—all that was available to us since there was no oil for the lamps. Besides, I was exhausted. Fully clothed, I collapsed upon a blanketless bed.

A pattern commenced the following morning which was to endure for five days. I would go into the village to purchase necessities; Le Rennet would alternately fish and nap. Sometimes I would join him by the river, but most often I dawdled about the cottage. Mayerling was a forbidden subject and our conversation, though companionable, was essentially of a trifling nature. He dreamed his dreams, and I dreamed mine. The room I had claimed obviously served Mallarme as both a bedchamber and study. Books, notes, and sketches were piled on a table, in boxes, along the walls. On the wall below the window hung three exquisite lithographs. One was a scene of Oriental voluptuousness; another was a spirited carnival piece. But the third was the source of my dreams: a divinely beautiful female head whose expression was provokingly indeterminate. Mery Laurent.

"Henri! Wilmot!" Can anyone imagine the thrill which coursed through me when I heard her voice, the voice of my dreams? There she was, gracefully alighting from a carriage. "Yes, it *is* me!" she laughed as I stood rooted to the steps. In a daze, I assisted her with her baggage, a single trunk and a small wooden case. "Well, what is it you say? Has the cat eaten your tongue?"

"Mery!" I managed, "how wonderful it is—"

"Ah, but I am not sure I approve, Wilmot. Perhaps I liked you better before." It was a confused moment before I realized that she was referring to my teeth. Once inside the cottage, I offered her my chamber, but she suggested that Le Rennet's might be more comfortable. Clearly she knew where the better mattress was.

He arrived from the river, having heard her calls. Mery's expression grew serious. "Henri, when I returned to Paris two days ago, this was waiting for me." She handed him a letter. "I convinced Stephane that it might be important, so he told me of your journey here."

As Le Rennet read the letter, I informed Mery of the events which had transpired during her absence. "Rats! Poor Wilmot," she said, stroking my cheek tenderly. "But what of Henri? Has he found the truth about Rudolph's death? Thomas did not know. Stephane did not know. Do you know, Wilmot?" About to answer, I was cut short by Le Rennet.

"Mery, how did you arrive in Valvins?"

"By carriage, naturally. Did you think I would walk?"

"From Jacques?" he asked.

"But of course. I always hire carriages from him."

"I believe we should leave Valvins," he said, quietly but ominously.

"What is it?" I asked.

"The letter purports to be from Baroness Metzengerstein. She warns me of the Baron's threat to use any means possible to prevent my communicating my theories to Their Majesties and disturbing the order and serenity of the Austrian Empire."

"It was kind of her to once more risk so much on our account."

"The letter is a forgery. Not only is it written in a masculine hand, not only would Ida Illyes eschew the term *order*, but also she is a Hungarian and her primary concern would not be the serenity of the *Austrian* Empire."

"The Baron? Mery was followed from Paris and has led him to our hideaway?"

"Unlikely. But when her carriage returns, a simple inquiry

into its destination, a few francs to the driver, and we will be exposed."

"Where shall we go?" I cried. Was I to spend the rest of my life pursued by the Baron?

"Anywhere, anywhere out of this world," the old man responded.

The evening repast was solemn. Le Rennet was absorbed in making plans, I presumed, while I found myself unable to think coherently. Mery tried to cheer us with chatter about her adventures in the countryside and about a new playwright who insisted on assaulting his audience both verbally and physically. She did not entirely succeed. I was enthralled by her presence but despondent, since it seemed likely we would again be parted. Yet it was because of a bit of gossip that the final details of Mayerling were disclosed.

"Have you heard? Baroness Vetsera left letters to her sister, to her mother, to several others. All are filled with deep, dark hints of love and death and escape. Some people see witchery in them. She is blamed for Rudolph's death. Everyone says terrible things about her."

Le Rennet turned on Mery. I was stunned, for although the old man could be crotchety or sarcastic, he was invariably polite with women. But now he lashed at Mery, berating her for listening to and perpetuating such filth. "The work of small minds! Damn them all, I will not have it! Of all the heart-aches our poor flesh is heir to, I have known none which is so universally melancholy—so tragic!—as the premature death of a beautiful young girl. She was only seventeen! No, by God, he shall not murder her twice!"

He began to clear the table. Silently, Mery arose and assisted him. As she took the last dish away, he patted her hand. "Griswold," he said, "I will need your help. I must write a letter to Elisabeth." Brooking no interruption, he dictated and I dutifully took down his words. Finally he instructed me to make a fair copy. While I labored, he spoke intimately with Mery. "Now read it to us," he said to me, when I at last put down my pen.

To Her Imperial and Royal Highness the Most Serene Lady the Empress Elisabeth:

It is with the greatest sadness that I find myself compelled to write this letter. Your Majesty's friendship, your generosity, your trust, deserve to be better rewarded. Since our meeting, I have learned that Sister Catherine, who claims to have received prophetic visions, has informed Your Majesty that Crown Prince Rudolph is not suffering the torments of the damned, that He was not a suicide. Our reasons differ, but I must agree with her.

Of the rising of tomorrow's sun—a probability that as yet lies in the future—I do not pretend to be one thousandth part as sure as I am of the irretrievably by-gone Fact! Although painful in the extreme, may I beg Your Majesty to recall certain facts about the tragedy at Mayerling?

Fact: The servant Loschek stated he heard no shots during the night of the tragedy, despite his close proximity to the room of the Crown Prince.

Fact: When entry was forced into the antechamber and a panel of the Prince's bedroom door was smashed, the same Loschek, upon glimpsing the scene, cried excitedly, 'They are both dead!'

Fact: It was Loschek alone who entered the Crown Prince's room, while both Count Hoyos and Prince Coburg waited in the antechamber.

Fact: Baroness Mary Vetsera died several hours before the Prince. She was undoubtedly shot by a small revolver, probably a Bulldog. She died instantly.

Fact: The condition of Baroness Vetsera's body, especially that of her left hand, disallows a conclusion of suicide.

Fact: Doctor Widerhofer briefly examined the scene at Mayerling shortly after the bodies were discovered. He recalls seeing a revolver next to the Crown Prince's body, yet none was later reported or found.

Again, I deeply regret disturbing Your Majesty with such unpleasant memories, but I must proceed. The dark of doubt must be dispelled.

Fact: A single shot from any known revolver could not have caused the wound to the Crown Prince's head.

Fact: The examination of the Prince's body was carried out in haste, under extreme pressure, and in an atmosphere of confusion.

Fact: A complete autopsy was not performed, the attending physicians limiting themselves to the Prince's cranium.

These facts and others drew me inexorably to one conclusion which the testimony of Father Degrote confirmed. Your Majesty, your son, the Crown Prince Rudolph, is alive. Yes, beyond doubt, physically alive. Yet—I must say this, Your Majesty—it would be better if he were actually dead, as all the world believes.

This is no hoax, Your Majesty, no cruel jest. For a moment, I beg that you suspend your disbelief.

Imagine, if you will, that a prince was born into an empire that was the glory of the world. He was reared in a palace which, despite its splendors, haunted him. Ghosts of the past subdued and frustrated his natural genius. Endless rounds of hollow ceremonial duties imprisoned him whose soul had out-grown his mortal position. The prince despaired.

Imagine, then, the joy of this young prince when in his travels he chanced upon another man who to an extraordinary degree resembled himself! As a prank, the young prince enlisted this double to take his place at one of those boring functions, one which most likely occurred in some remote part of the empire. It was a challenge to the prince.

Could he coach the double to such a point where no one would detect the deception? He could. He did. (Has not Your Majesty done the same thing, costumed your hairdresser in your garb, allowing the crowds to pay homage to her while you amused yourself elsewhere, unrecognized and undisturbed?) Again, and yet again, the double was substituted for the real prince. To insure the ready acceptance of his counterfeit, the prince systematically developed eccentricities of behavior and of grooming. More, he deliberately trained his double in these mannerisms, trained him to copy this self-caricature the real prince created.

But the prince grew dissatisfied with boyish pranks. His brain was in ferment; ideas and ideals were supplied by his education and his own experience. The revolutions in America and France. The uprisings of 1848. Garibaldi and his thousand. More and more the prince rebelled against the ghosts of the past which still held sway. He embraced the spectre of the future, seeing his mission as that of a midwife to a new world, rejecting entirely the old, caring nothing for what would replace it, as long as it proved different. As others before him, the prince adopted a motto: before one can build, one must destroy.

But now imagine that the position of the prince is so circumscribed, his movements are so closely watched, that he is powerless. He broods and remembers the success of his double in deceiving even casual acquaintances, subordinates, and the public. The imposter could never deceive a member of the family or an intimate acquaintance. Not alive, that is. But as a corpse? Partially disfigured? A corpse whose discovery would excite the greatest confusion? It is possible, decides the prince. So slowly, carefully, he plots to remove himself from the world, yet live.

The plan is simplicity itself. The real prince will leave his country, the double left in his place. The double will then be lured to a remote location where he will fall victim to a fatal accident. But the prince meets a beautiful young girl. Coldly he calculates that her presence would add a touch of verisimilitude to his stage-craft. The prince abandons his plan of death by misadventure and adopts a new and more sinister one: a romantically inspired double suicide. How much more confusion will surround any official investigation? How much more quickly will authorities move to put an end to the entire matter? Most important, they will ask the wrong question: why? rather than who?

The girl is told of the double's existence and is introduced to him. The prince promises her that they will run off together while the double remains to occupy the attention of the rest of the world, at least for a long enough period to insure their escape. What more logical choice for a destination than exotic Egypt where the young girl spent some happy years? They will meet there to begin their life together. The prince precedes her to Port Said. On that fatal evening the young girl arrives, expecting to be spirited away to join her royal lover. Instead, she is joined forever to her Maker.

The news of the deaths of the prince and his mistress shocks the world. The real prince returns from Egypt by ship, arrives at Brindisi, and makes his way to Fiume. There, his friend and co-conspirator, an archduke totally in sympathy with the prince's aims, gives him shelter and assists him in carrying out the rest of his plan.

Yet on board ship, the prince performed a most daring and foolhardy act. He inquired of a priest if the latter was aware of the prince's suicide. Why the prince made this query, we can only speculate. Did he decide to add one more touch of obfuscation? To leave a hint of his own existence, which he knew would be reported, as a kind of twit of the official nose? Was he overly excited, losing track of the dates? Was there an error in timing which caused the double assassination to be carried out later than originally planned? Or was the prince so deeply engaged in celebrating his own death, that the wine overtook him and he became careless? Whatever the reason, it was a dangerous move, one which the prince may live to regret.

Your Majesty, I beg you not to dismiss my little fable as the ravings of a senile mind or the concoction of a vile hoaxer.

Why were Count Hoyos and Prince Coburg invited to Mayerling on the day the bodies were discovered? As has happened, were they not the witnesses needed to confirm the circumstances surrounding the two deaths? Loschek could not report hearing shots during the night, since he was instructed to summon witnesses who would verify by their testimony what he knew awaited them behind that dread door. And Coburg did not arrive at Mayerling until the following morning.

What caused Loschek to make the precipitous remark, "They are both dead"? What did he see as he looked into that room? I suggest, Your Majesty, that he saw that the double of the Crown Prince was not dead! Despite a bullet which Loschek had fired through the man's skull from one of the Prince's personal revolvers, the man moved. He lived. When Loschek alone entered the room to affirm the condition of the pair, he seized a bottle of champagne and completed the job he had begun the night before. He savagely smashed in the skull of the impostor.

And who but the ever-present Loschek could have removed the revolver which Dr. Widerhofer reported seeing?

The shot itself would have made recognition of the impostor unlikely. The shattering of the skull made it highly improbable. The hysterical state of the Hofburg, when the autopsy was performed, made it impossible.

If not for the purpose of substituting a double, Your Majesty, how else is one to explain the extreme changes in the appearance, disposition and behavior of the Crown Prince during these last years? Why would someone forge a page in the pharmacy record book at the Hofburg? Obviously, to disguise the prescription and use of particular drugs by the real Crown Prince. Otherwise suspicions might be aroused if traces of them were not found in the body of the impostor, or if the impostor did not possess the conditions for which the drugs were prescribed. And that name, Your Majesty, *Vicomte de Montreine*. Few men without the Prince's background could have chosen one which was so appropriate yet non-extant.

Once again, I beg Your Majesty, do not ignore my cautionary little tale; in special heed its moral. The Crown Prince has set a course which makes him an outcast, forever shunned or hunted like Cain himself. His very soul was ever bi-partite. And now, in his zealous pursuit of his cause, he has found that synthesis which he lacked. His abnormal excitation and his impotency are now combined to achieve one end. He has not forgotten the slights, the insults, suffered at the hands of the aristocracy, most of whom he despised for their ignorance, their crudity. He has not forgotten the frustration of inactivity, while his fine powers lay rusting. And now his cause is revenge, not simply in some intrigue to seize the Austrian throne and thus avenge himself upon his father, and his tormentors at the court. It is much more sinister, Your Majesty, for the Crown Prince has declared a holy war against all monarchy, against all existing governments! And especially against the past itself.

I once wrote a fiction about a man who was used up. I have lived to see my own cherished country similarly exhausted, its fine moral aims depleted. Now, I fear, I am witnessing an entire epoch, a whole world being used up, destroyed. Take heed, Your Most Gracious Majesty. We may laugh, but we shall smile no more.

Your most loyal and obedient servant,
Henri Le Rennet, Esq.

It was Mery who finally broke the silence. *"Fantastique.* Did I not tell you Henri could—" she paused, "—but it cannot be. Rudolph, alive? Impossible."

"All too possible," said Le Rennet. He folded the final draft of his letter and sealed it within an envelope, which in turn was sealed in another.

"Will you mail your theories to Her Majesty?" I asked.

"Mail? She would never receive this letter through the usual means. It must be delivered to her in person."

"But how are we to do that?"

"Not we, Griswold. This task is mine alone. It is time we parted." Though it was twenty minutes after midnight, he prepared to take his leave and we could not shake him from his resolve. We assisted him as best we could. At the last minute, Mery placed a flask of brandy in his case. The three of us stood in the shadows beyond the cottage.

Le Rennet embraced Mery, speaking very softly to her. Then, still holding her hand, he stepped back and bowed. "But of course I shall miss you, my dear Mery. You represent all that is the best of France—her art, her poise, her charm, her defiance, her wit. And of course," he chuckled, "her sublime naughtiness."

"But Henri! You will return to France, to *les mardistes.* We will sit, you and I, and listen to Stephane's poetry. He is composing a new poem, about my hair. You will adore it."

"Perhaps. Someday." He kissed her hand. *"Au revoir."* Mery ran to the cottage, a small sob escaping her.

"And you, Master Griswold. My profoundest thanks. May life bring you a great deal more good fortune, and a little more good sense. Goodbye, my friend." He embraced me in the French fashion, gently brushing his lips upon my cheeks, and disappeared down the path and into the night.

"Goodbye, sir!" I cried. *"Et bonne chance!"* I felt tears in my eyes and a kind of emptiness in my heart. I had never contemplated our eventual parting. Had I done so, it would have been pictured differently: in anger, perhaps, from the unshakable conviction that I was indeed in the hands of a hoaxer; in laughter and gaiety, perhaps, as we celebrated the irrefutable solution of *l'affaire Mayerling*; in sorrow, perhaps, for an old man upon his sick bed, his mind lost to us, his body near defeat. But not this parting: sudden, almost casual, yet touched by surreptiousness and urgency. Most of all, a parting which seemed incomplete. Yet I knew that he was right. My world was not his; my life lay elsewhere, at home.

But how was I to get there? *Good fortune,* the old man had said. I desperately needed it. My hopes for the Exposition had been dashed. In the months of my sojourn I had received but one order for Bob's Oil—hardly enough to reimburse me for the loss of my sample cases, let alone the monstrous expenses I had incurred.

I fled to Marseilles and for two days hid in a dingy hotel while an officious bank clerk made lengthy inquiries before endorsing my letter of credit. At any moment I expected a clutch of *gendarmes* to seize me and drag me off to a dungeon.

Or perhaps a worse fate would overtake me. An item in a newspaper seemed to confirm that fear. Had the names *Le Rennet* and *Valvins* not appeared, I would have overlooked it. The son of the apothecary had been engaged by a stranger to deliver a parcel to a M. Le Rennet. Since Le Rennet was not at home, the youth had returned with the package, depositing it in the rear of the shop. Later, when he attempted to chase a cat who was nosing around it, the package exploded, seriously injuring the boy. The Police were mystified. A search was underway for Le Rennet and a companion, a foreigner.

At last the funds were approved and I booked the first passage I could find to America. I was forced to share the only available cabin aboard a freight hauler with two immigrants, from Russia, I believe they said. They constantly demanded that I teach them our country's language, holding up a shoe, a brush, a hat or miming various actions. They desisted only when a storm attacked us midway through our crossing. All three of us were very ill. However, when we arrived in New York, two days behind schedule, I discovered that one of them had been well enough to steal my watch.

In Baltimore again, safely ensconced in the Griswold Medical Dispensary, I was extremely busy, so much so that my foreign adventure temporarily receded into the background, except for one day, the recollection of which continues to glow in my memory.

It was the afternoon following Le Rennet's departure from Valvins. We had some hours to wait before Mery could make a connection with a common stage carriage to take her back to Paris. We were picnicking together when a sudden spring shower forced us to seek shelter in an abandoned boat-house.

"Wilmot, do you think Henri really believes Rudolph is alive?" she asked, tumbling her damp flaming hair about her shoulders, trying to pat it dry with a kerchief.

"I am sure the old fellow believes the Crown Prince is alive. But is he? I do not know."

"But that makes it so difficult. I mean our wager. . . ." I at once assured her that I would be a cad to press such an ambiguous situation to its conclusion. "Aha! You do not find me attractive?" She pouted.

"Indeed I do. Extraordinarily attractive." I went on in that vein, mentioning the painting I had seen at the Baron's.

"Ah, Edouard. Yes, he was a genius. Only this year are those donkeys at the Academy awakening to that. Six years after he died! Did you like the painting, Wilmot?" I confessed that although it was beautiful I had found it rather embarrassing. She scolded me. "Artists grow accustomed to their models; they see them as nothing more than shape or color."

"Then I could never become a painter."

She laughed gaily, kicking off her shoes. "But that depends on the model, *n'est-ce pas?*" I protested, but not vigorously. My work as the old man's *brosseur* had definitely come to an end.

L'ENVOI

NEW YEAR'S MORNING. MONDAY, 1900. I HAVE TAKEN UP cigars, and I plan to enjoy one before retiring. They are an expensive and, to some, an immoral habit. I find them most satisfying. I wonder if the Baroness, wherever she might be, still smokes? Have her teeth been stained like mine? Now my artificial teeth are indistinguishable from my natural ones. My mirror also shows deepening lines of age and other changes in my features which might, I confess, be attributed to an excessive consumption of Le Rennet's tomato concoction. I have introduced the potion to some intimate friends who have praised its tang and medicinal virtues. His gumbo is similarly acclaimed.

Last evening I presided over a *reveillon* which I held for some of my employees. Because it was Sunday, I ended the festivities early, despite the blandishments of younger guests who suggested we adjourn elsewhere to make a carouse in welcome of the New Year. I declined, and in a state of mingled sadness and inexplicable anxiety, I repaired to my study. From my desk, I secured my *cahier* with its fading blue cover and the few notes which I had managed to rescue. Once again, I opened the old ledger. I determined, in that last hour of 1899, to complete my account of those *bizarre* months in Paris. I have written the night away, and it is all put down now, or nearly all.

I am moved to acknowledge that for some months I was obsessed with Mery Laurent. I wrote her countless letters. Since I had never known her address in Paris—or anywhere else—I posted them in care of Evans. Later, in care of M. Mallarme. Receiving no reply, I finally wrote directly to the dentist himself. Some months later, I received a short missive. Curtly he told me that Mery was well and extremely busy. He was extremely busy also. To my appended query about the servant Loschek, he supplied this answer. Shortly after the death of Rudolph, Johann Loschek retired from service at court, having been granted a small pension. Then, he disappeared. In any event, for nearly a decade now, my memories of Mery have not been obsessive. They are fond. And although I do not pretend to understand Mr. Keats' poem, I feel as his narrator, that Mery cannot fade. She is held in memory, unchanged.

The year of 1890 brought two incidents to my attention which I found curious, if not sinister, in their import. Sometime after the event (Baltimore newspapers are tardy in reporting upon foreign matters), I learned that on October 8, 1889, the very year of Rudolph's death, Archduke Johann Salvator voluntarily renounced his title and all rights pertaining thereto. He adopted a commoner's name, Johann Orth, and immediately left Austria. He had simply refused to remain a Hapsburg! Later, Salvator, or Orth, was reported killed in a shipwreck while circumnavigating Cape Horn. No trace of the ship or the man was ever found. However, rumors have arisen. From time to time, reliable people have claimed to have seen him in the Americas. Some say he was recruiting an army of mercenaries.

That same year, 1890, one of my travelling men related this story to me. The newspapers in Pennsylvania were carrying a warning directed at recent European immigrants, especially those of Slovene ancestry. An imposter, claiming to be Crown Prince Rudolph, was canvassing the immigrant population, attempting to raise funds to support an army which he would lead against the Empire. According to some who met this impostor, he did bear a striking resemblance to the late Prince.

And one thing else. Among the hail of holiday greetings that I received that year was a short notice which had been clipped from a Paris newspaper. It was mailed from Greece and contained no hint of the sender—simply "Merry Christmas" printed across the page bottom. I translated it as best I could and learned that Baron Frederick Metzengerstein of the Austrian Embassy had been kidnapped by a band of footpads. No word was heard of him for one week, when the Baroness received a note informing her of the Baron's whereabouts. The note was signed: *Montressor.*

The Baron was discovered, following the note's instructions, in the hold of an abandoned river barge which had run aground some distance from Paris. He was barely alive, having survived the week with nothing but bilge-water and putrid heads of cabbage which his abductors had left him. The Baron was in a highly disturbed state of mind. During his captivity he was set upon by huge water rats which infested the barge. According to Alexandre Etienne, Prefect of the Paris Police, every effort was being made to discover his abductors. Were Etienne's efforts so intensive? I do not know, but I hope they failed. I read the report without a twinge of proper Christian sentiment. In fact, with some pleasure. While I drank one of Le Rennet's concoctions, I was reminded of a short story by Edgar Allan Poe, "The Cask of Amontillado." Could it be?

I was blessed with eight years of prosperous tranquillity during which the events of Paris were mostly submerged by the pleasures and demands of commerce. But in 1898, tragedy struck, as usual in triple. In the summer of that year, my mother, Sarah Griswold, departed from this earth. Before she succumbed, she informed me that she had learned certain facts which caused her to repent naming me after my uncle Rufus. With the aid of Mr. George Woodburry and others, I later investigated her statements, and found that Le Rennet's charges against my uncle were substantially true. Rufus W. Griswold, as the literary executor and biographer of Edgar Allan Poe, behaved in a most dastardly fashion, falsifying facts to tarnish the memory of that great poet. I was sickened. It was as though I had been betrayed from beyond the grave by a past which I had not created yet one in which I had implicitly believed.

I had not recovered from this shock when another arrived. Our newspapers talked of little else for weeks. On September tenth, the Empress Elisabeth was assassinated. Her assailant was one Luigi Lucheni, a former body servant to the Prince of Aragon. Lucheni was also a well-known anarchist. The police were uncertain whether he had acted alone or in a conspiracy with others. Nor could Lucheni offer a satisfactory account of why he had come to Geneva, how he knew Her Majesty would be there, or how he knew her habits well enough to approach and kill her.

Even now, in retrospect, the thought is chilling. Loschek? Or had Rudolph himself conspired in the death of his own mother? The thought is too monstrous. The sad eyes stare back at me from my charcoal sketch. No, it cannot be.

The third tragedy had actually struck earlier, but I did not so quickly get news of it. Stephane Mallarme had died on the afternoon of September ninth, just a day before Elisabeth. He suffered a seizure while vacationing at his cottage in Valvins. Sadly I recalled the kindnesses he had shown me and wrote my condolences to his family. From his daughter Genevieve, I received a note of thanks. Also of polite regret to my request for any accounts her late father left concerning Le Rennet. On his death-bed, her father had insisted that all notes and papers be destroyed. She had complied fully with his dying wish.

Le Rennet. I have omitted recounting the frustrations I experienced in attempting to determine his identity. I did discover that a Henry R. Reynolds was a Fourth Ward judge for the Congressional election held in Baltimore on October 3, 1849. And that Winfield Scott of New Jersey was nominated for the Presidency by the Whig Party on the twentieth of June, 1852. He was roundly defeated by Franklin Pierce. But these are commonplace facts. Concerning the fantastic claims of the old man, I have learned nothing which would allow me to reason my way to a firm conclusion.

No matter. I see him now, across the years, an old and frail man holding himself together, keeping himself alive, by some indescribable, incredible power of will. A man of fiery temperament and extraordinary wit. A man of essential kindness. And just. Whither he travelled upon our departure, I cannot know for certain. But, alas, he must surely by now have made his final journey. May his dreams be sweet, his mind in repose. This year I will again visit the grave of Edgar Allan Poe. Who lies there? I have often thought that the answer is unimportant. I have stood there in the dusk to pay homage to a friend.

It has been light for an hour, now. Is this the New Century's beginning. The dawn of a new era? I fear I have lost interest in the question. For me, the new era began when the old one ended, on a snowswept night in Paris. And like my friend, I feel that I, too, have outlived an age, an era which shall nevermore return. As for the future, I can but remember his lines:

> *The night, tho clear, shall frown,*
> *And the stars shall not look down.*

FINI